SECOND CHANCE
SOLDIER

MICHELE E. GWYNN

AN M.E. GWYNN PUBLICATION

CONTENTS

TERMS

Terms

414th Nesher Field Intelligence Battalion, Gaza sector: Nesher is an Israeli word for 'vulture.' The 414th is the Southern Command Battalion in the Gaza sector for the Israeli Defense Force or IDF.

PATCH-COM: PATCH refers to "Patch 'em up," a phrase denoting the work of military field medics working to temporarily patch up wounds on injured soldiers in battle. PATCH-COMMAND is a *fictional unit* where wounded soldiers are sent to be patched up and put back into action.

PTSD: Post Traumatic Stress Disorder

SOCOM: USSOCOM is the United States Special Operations Command at MacDill Air Force Base in Tampa, Florida.

Task Force Sword: This is the designation for Special Operations Forces sent in to pursue high-value targets in Afghanistan and Iraq since October 2001 in response to the attack on U.S. soil September 11, 2001.

GET A FREE BOOK

Get a FREE BOOK (or two) from Michele E. Gwynn. See my website for details. micheleegwynnauthor.com,

Like FREE audiobooks? Check out my YouTube channel and enjoy full length audiobooks from my Harvest Trilogy (scifi) and Angelic Hosts series (Romantic Fantasy). More coming soon in my military romance series. SUBSCRIBE to my YouTube channel to receive alerts when I upload the next free audiobook. (And share this info with your audiobook-loving friends). Visit my YouTube channel at @MicheleEGwynnAuthor.

Cover by Emeegee Graphics, Cover photo (soldier) by AdobeStock 64168582 Extended license, and Playa del Carmen photo by Keenan Barber (Unsplash). PATCH-COM logo copyright (C) Michele E. Gwynn.

Editing: M.E. Gwynn

Formatting: M.E. Gwynn

INTRODUCTION

Dearest Reader,

I hope you're enjoying The Soldiers of PATCH-COM. This series was born from two places; one is my deepest gratitude to those who serve, who give so much to protect our country, our freedom, and the other is from my own experience living with a physical handicap. All my life, doctors and random people tried to tell me what I couldn't do, wouldn't be able to do, because of a childhood diagnosis of Rheumatoid Arthritis. Sure, it has been a struggle, but despite it all, I've overcome so many roadblocks. I was told I would be bedridden by high school. I'm still walking (and dancing now and again). I was told I would most likely die before I could graduate. Well... I walked the stage with my classmates and went on to college earning my degree in applied sciences. I was told I would never be able to drive.

Phht! Of course I can drive! I was told I would never be able to learn to type with my arthritic hands. I type around sixty words a minute. Was told I would never be able to live alone. Ha! I moved out at twenty-one. Now, I take care of my mother who selflessly took care of me while I went through the toughest trials a child could face.

By some miracle, the arthritis went into remission around the age of 20-21, and has stayed dormant. Lucky me. I've worked in healthcare, education, and journalism, all before embarking on a career as an author of fiction. I'd say I've done rather well beating the odds.

Which leads me to our amazing wounded warriors who do not know the word 'quit'.

Once a soldier, always a soldier, and the team of my fictional world of PATCH-COM exemplify the courage, the tenacity, and the dedication to service I've witnessed in all my family and friends who serve/have served. I come from a military family, and I am so proud of each and every one of them.

It is from these two experiences that this team of ragtag special forces operators came to life between the pages. So, welcome to Camp Lazarus, and to PATCH-COM. Enjoy the ride.

~ Michele

CHAPTER 1

Gerry 'Mac' Maclean stared at the picture on the wall. In it, a group of twenty-two men faced the camera, arms slung around each other's shoulders. Their faces were dirty, their uniforms covered in soot, and in some cases, blood splatter and bone fragments. With high-powered rifles slung over their shoulders, they stood together in the middle of a clearing in what was left of the small village inside Syria. Around them, nothing but rubble and in the background, black smoke rose up obscuring the blue of the sky. Some of the men were smiling but the expressions on the faces of the others revealed no emotion at all. The casual observer wouldn't see the problem with this stillness, but Mac knew. He knew because he lived it. He was one of the men in the picture, and he was not smiling. The horror of that one day traumatized him so deeply, he had never quite recovered. He knew, looking at those men, each an Army Airborne Ranger, elite soldiers trained to be the best anywhere in the world, that several of them had been broken beyond repair that day. He knew the reason for that black plume of smoke in the background. Still remembered the distinct stench. Still heard the screams in his nightmares. The wailing of a terrified child...

He'd lost friends that day, not to bullets, but to madness. His unit, a tight band of brothers, had been joined by Syrian freedom fighters. Most were half-trained non-military men devoted to taking their country back from Assad, but the enemy wasn't just the Assad regime. There were Islamic fundamentalists among them, ISIS fighters trying to get a foothold in the battle. They were vicious and did not follow any honorable rules of engagement. They killed anyone in their path—opposition armies, civilians, women, even children. By the time his unit arrived on scene, the rogue group of ISIS fighters had destroyed the village and killed nearly everyone in it. Mac came upon a small child, a girl about three years old with big brown eyes crying over the body of her dead mother. The girl looked at him with such fear, it tore at his heart. He squatted down trying to gently beckon her over and away from the body. Just as she took her first tentative step toward him, a shot rang out and the child fell face-first into the dirt. Her cries forever silenced.

With no time to react, he sighted the shooter on a rooftop—a man wearing a black keffiyeh—aimed and fired. The man's body tumbled over the edge, a fine red mist engulfing him. Only then, did he realize he was running to the child. He scooped her up and ran for cover, but there was no longer any need. She was already gone. When the battle was over, he was the one to place her and her mother in the large pit. He laid the child atop the mother's chest, her cheek resting on her mother's shoulder. Together in life, reunited in death. He walked away then, not wanting to see the first flames rising consuming the accelerant thrown atop the dead.

A journalist with the BBC arrived catching only the tail end of the battle. It was he who asked Mac's captain to pose for a picture. He hyped it as the American military liberating another village of oppressed citizens, another win in the war. But Mac knew it was all bullshit. The war was unwinnable. Winning wasn't in the best interests of the governments involved, but a sustained war was good for elections. He'd watched over the years as governments changed hands from good leaders to greedy, power-hungry bastards. He knew the score, and after seeing the light go out of that child's eyes, something inside him died. It was the piece of his soul that held him together, and without it, he fell apart.

Sucked into the labyrinth of old memories, Mac rubbed the third finger on his left hand. The emptiness there yet another reminder of all he had lost.

Post-traumatic stress sent him into a spiral and the army, through a series of colossal fuckups, sent him here. To Camp Lazarus. To a top-secret unit of wounded warriors known to a select few as PATCH-COM. Stranger still than an elite unit of broken soldiers was the location of Camp Lazarus—the infamous AREA 51 in Nevada.

It was here, deep within the bowels of a mountain, he finally found some peace.

Therapy sessions with Dr. Delaney did not originally go well. Mac barely uttered a word then. He knew that his communication skills hadn't improved...much...but when Major Lila Delaney handed him a yellow pack of seeds one afternoon and suggested he plant them in a pot, it changed everything. Dumbfounded as to why she gave them to him, he looked at her like she'd lost her mind.

"They're zinnias. Put them in dirt. Water them." She looked down then and wrote a few short notes.

"Water?" Mac stared at her and then at the small yellow package of seeds.

"Yes, Sergeant, they require water to grow."

In his mind, Mac raged. *Is this the best the military has to offer by way of help? Tips on gardening? First, I'm sent to the wrong facility, and now this? Fuck me! I won't do it. Planting a bunch of damned seeds isn't going to stop the nightmares, won't fix what's broken, won't bring her back!*

His face contorted into a mask of confusion and anger. The latter was palpable, but Dr. Delaney sat calmly regarding the soldier before her. Her hard, brown eyes did not waver, and she never flinched when he blew up. She was the toughest woman Mac had ever encountered and she didn't take any of his shit. It was one of the reason's he developed a grudging respect for her. The other reason was that her mannish behavior threw him for a loop. He never quite knew whether to call her ma'am or sir, but he never failed to salute.

He took the pack of seeds and left her office. They sat on his desk for a week. Every time he walked into his room, there they were, a bright yellow packet with colorful flowers displayed on the front, a constant reminder of Dr. Delaney's order.

"Plant them," he grumbled to himself. "Where the hell am I to do that here?" Being several stories underground, there was nowhere in which he could plant them where they might receive sunlight. And as far as he was aware, there was no dirt, or even a designated garden area.

On the seventh day, he finally gave in. Grabbing the bright packet, he headed out and back down the hall. Finding the nearest low-level Private, he barked out an order.

"Find a bucket, a hammer, a nail, and some dirt. Don't care how or where. Just do it!"

The Private, a young man no more than nineteen years of age and fresh out of basic training, eyed the volatile-looking Mac nervously bobbing his head, his feet already backing away to fulfill the order. "Sir, yes sir. Right away sir!"

Within the hour, Mac had his supplies in hand. He applied the nail to the bottom of the bucket hammering five drain holes through the metal. Then he poured the dirt inside, rich Nevada soil obtained from the mountain above. He eyed the yellow packet and then ripped the top open. The instructions on the back said to plant the seeds one inch down into the dirt. He did so carefully, spacing them out until all the seeds were planted. Then he opened his bottled water and poured the liquid over the top. When it began seeping through the drain holes and spilling out onto his desk, he cursed, looking around for something to sit the small bucket on. There was nothing available, so he sat it in the sink. Later, he filched a large plate from the cafeteria. It became the catch-all for the bucket.

The problem of sunlight, however, evaded him until he remembered when he'd first arrived at Camp Lazarus. The same Private he terrorized for gardening supplies had been the one who explained about the lights in his bedroom. There were UV lights for daytime to help with the loss of natural light and Tungsten lighting for night to help regulate the body's natural Circadian rhythm. All he had to do was sit the bucket beneath one of the lights, one of which happened to be over his desk. He placed it neatly on the corner and watched it every day. On the third day, the seeds sprouted. It made him strangely happy to see something growing in the otherwise desolate room. When the first flowers bloomed, he smiled. The smile was quickly smothered, but inside, Mac felt the first inkling of peace. That was then. Now, he had an entire area within the compound dedicated for his personal use—and it was filled with flowers, bushes, and a couple of trees. Mac's garden became a point of interest, one that drew the other soldiers to the doorway looking inside with wonder. At first, no one dared enter, but with Dr. Delaney's encouragement, Mac begrudgingly allowed the new patients to come in. He even created a couple of seating areas where they could convalesce among the flora and fauna.

The soldiers were still afraid of Mac, but his outbursts lessoned eventually becoming somewhat manageable. Working in his garden became his coping mechanism and sharing what he created brought him a certain amount of joy. Seeing the wounded warriors with so much trauma in their eyes come into the space he created and marveling at the lushness while it worked its magic soothing their souls felt like redemption. In helping himself, he found a way to help his brothers in arms. But they weren't allowed to pick the flowers! One found out the hard way and was banished from the garden for a week.

The memory brought a small smirk to his lips and his hazel eyes twinkled. He ran a hand over his shaved head and turned to find Eastwood standing in the doorway.

"The Major wants us in the conference room ASAP," he said.

Mac nodded. Sergeant Harold Tyler, codename Eastwood, had become a close friend over the past year. When he arrived at Camp Lazarus, he was in bad shape having lost half his left leg to an RPG explosion in Kuwait. Mac noted then that Eastwood was as tough as one would expect from a Spec Ops soldier. A Green Beret weapons specialist, the Sergeant already had an impressive record. Now, he was a member of PATCH-COM. A broken soldier put back together by technology and willpower, he proved himself once again to be the fighter the army trained him to be. Over time, he became Mac's friend and the newly wedded husband of their bio-tech designer, Joely Winter Tyler.

Since the wedding, Eastwood lived off base two hours south in northern Las Vegas. The fact that he'd been called in meant something was up.

"Details?" Mac asked.

"I know as much as you, Mac, which is nothing. Come on, let's grab the fellas." He stepped aside and waited as Mac walked through the door joining him in the hallway.

"Art's with Janeway," Mac mumbled.

Art Diaz was one of two men brought to Camp Lazarus on the same C-5 transport as Eastwood. An army sniper, Art had lost an eye, but gained a new one tricked out with specialized laser-sighting. Natalie Janeway was Joely's communications specialist and all-around computer nerd. Many thought her too young for the job, but what she lacked in years, she more than made up with quiet competence. Art caught Natalie's eye and she kept him in her sights while going about her duties. Having one eye seemed to have put Art Diaz at a disadvantage because despite the puppy-eyed looks she cast his way, he had not noticed her…until Eastwood's wedding. A Versace gown and a good push-up bra had done what no amount of subtlety could, opened Art's eye. There was an open bet on when the two would finally close the deal since.

"What?" Eastwood's step faltered and he caught himself. He looked at Mac. "With, as in…" he gestured crudely.

Mac glared at him sideways. "Her room."

"Oh, shit!" Eastwood stroked his beard.

"Don't get too excited," said Mac. "He still ain't asked her out."

"Wait. You just said he is in her room. If they aren't doing the deed, then what's he doing there?"

Mac grunted. "Dancing."

Eastwood stopped. "What? You're messing with me now, Mac."

Mac paused, looking at the man. "Nope. Not."

Eastwood glared at Mac, waiting for an explanation.

A snort much like that of an irritated bull erupted from Mac's flared nostrils as he muttered, "Teaching him to waltz."

Eastwood let that sink in. He wasn't one to gossip, but right now, he'd give anything for Mac's usual monosyllabic answers to be full-throated, gushing teenage girl details. "She's teaching him to waltz?"

Mac nodded and headed back down the hall once again. Eastwood stood stock still a moment longer and then put his legs into motion catching up. They needed to find Jackson. Ben, Matt, and Nastjia. Getting information out of Mac was painful, but the others would tell him just what the hell was going on. Especially Jackson Hicks. The guitar-strumming cowboy loved to ramble, and Eastwood knew this was too juicy not to share. Plus, he had money riding on it. The bet began just a few months after they arrived at Camp Lazarus and had evolved as betting deadlines were missed. Eastwood was now two thousand in and the pot had grown to over ten thousand. The way he figured it; he could get all the money back that he bet on those missed dates and times if he ultimately won the bet. But he needed to know what was really going on inside Natalie Janeway's bedroom.

꧁꧂

The conference room was full. Their commander, Major Sydelle Maxwell, stood at the head of the table. The tall black woman had the straightest posture Mac had ever seen, which was impressive considering the injuries she sustained. A decorated army Black Hawk pilot, Maxwell had lost half her left arm and suffered multiple broken bones including a broken back when her helicopter was shot down. It took over a year and more surgeries than Mac could count for her to heal. A scar over her left eye cut through the eyebrow giving the Major a distinctive, badass look. In her fatigues, one barely noticed the bio-mechanical arm prosthetic she wore. He noticed early on she kept a glove on that hand. Despite all she went through, she came out the other side of it stronger.

Mac arrived at camp not long after Syd. He remembered watching the woman tough it out in physical therapy sessions inside the gym, but she never once quit, and she never cried. Now and again she eyed Mac as he pumped iron and climbed the rock wall. One afternoon she called him over.

"Front and center, Sergeant," she ordered.

Without hesitation, Mac dropped the fifty-pound bar-bells he was curling and approached, standing at attention. "Ma'am, yes ma'am," he saluted.

She cocked her head sideways as she leaned on her crutches, only two weeks post-op from back surgery. "At ease, Sergeant."

Mac immediately loosened his stance clasping his hands behind his back, his eyes staring straight ahead.

"Why are you here?" she asked.

"Ma'am?" The question confused him. "You summoned me, ma'am."

"That's not what I meant. Why are you here at Camp Lazarus? You look remarkably healthy."

Mac blinked. "Paperwork screw up, ma'am. Was supposed to be sent to Walter Reed, ma'am."

Major Maxwell's left eyebrow shot up tilting the scar into a wicked angle. "What's your damage, soldier?"

Mac hesitated. He didn't like talking about what was going on inside his head when he still didn't understand it himself. He shrugged, mumbling, "PTSD, ma'am."

She considered him carefully. "Some scars aren't visible," she replied. "What's your name, soldier?"

This one was easy to answer. "Gerry Maclean, 3rd Battalion, 75th Ranger Regiment."

"Airborne, eh? Your battalion aided Deltas in Task Force Sword in 2001. You were one of the three hundred sent into Afghanistan?"

"I was, ma'am." Memories flooded his head. Sweat broke out on his forehead as he tried to hold himself together. He didn't want to fall apart in front of the Major. Behind him, another soldier hooted loudly as he dropped a barbell onto the concrete floor. The resulting bang reverberated inside the gym and Mac began to shake.

Concern flooded Major Maxwell's eyes. "Joe," she said, calling out to the therapist approaching them, "Sergeant Maclean could use a break, I think."

Joe Poole, a middle-aged man with thinning salt and pepper hair wearing wire-rimmed glasses looked at Mac. Sweat ran down his face from his shaved scalp and his hazel eyes took on the expression of a cornered animal. Joe recognized the panic attack coming on and attempted to gently lead Mac away out of the gym, but he would not budge.

"Mac," said Joe, "it's okay. Come with me. We'll go see Dr. Delaney."

Mac struggled to speak. "Not...dismissed," he ground out through now-chattering teeth.

Major Maxwell marveled at the will power the sergeant exhibited even as his mind threatened to break. She snapped a salute. "Dismissed, Sergeant."

Relief washed over him for one brief moment as the Major released him from where he stood frozen to the spot. "Thank you, ma'am," he whispered, pain in every word.

Joe Poole led Mac away, but every afternoon thereafter, Major Maxwell and Sergeant Gerry 'Mac' Maclean shared their physical therapy session with Joe Poole, and over time, mutual respect grew. When the paperwork finally came through correcting the army's error and redirecting Mac to Walter Reed, it was Maxwell herself who stepped in to cancel the order. Mac had made great progress at Camp Lazarus, and now, he didn't want to go. And Major Maxwell saw no good reason to fix what wasn't broken. Taking Mac away from the place he had grown to feel safe within would set back that progress. Dr. Delaney agreed. On that day, Mac became an official member of PATCH-COM. He was forever grateful.

His gratitude and admiration for the Major was the foundation for his loyalty to her.

Next to Major Maxwell, his teammates assembled one by one around the table. Nastjia Moreno; was the first female Navy SEAL. She lost a foot in a boat rotor accident on her first mission. Then there was Ben 'Doc' Holiday, a Green Beret medic who'd suffered a badly broken leg which had since healed; Jackson 'Junkyard' Hicks, a Marine sniper who survived enemy fire that temporarily paralyzed his lower body now supported by an impressive right-leg exoskeleton support brace. He had the same laser-sighting prosthetic eye as Art. Next was Matt Rogers, a one-armed army bomb specialist. Last but not least, and late to the party was the subject of his conversation with Eastwood, Art Diaz, a one-eyed army sniper missing a couple of fingers on his right hand. Fortunately, not his trigger finger. These were the ones he knew and knew well. To his surprise three more men entered the conference room behind Art, taking their seats.

One was swarthy looking with a big nose and a shaved dome like Mac's. He wore a black t-shirt with camo pants and black boots. The man carried a sand-colored beret under his left arm as he limped, his face screwed up with a combination of pain and determination. The second was tall, slender, with high cheekbones and a square jaw. His ruddy complexion looked like it rarely saw the sun. This one wore MTP, multi-terrain pattern fatigues. He leaned on a cane and one arm was in a sling. The last man was shorter with dark hair and almost pretty features. He did not appear to have any injuries, but Mac knew that some war wounds weren't visible. He estimated the man stood at about 5'11", which, in this roomful of men, made him the short straw; excluding Nastjia, of course. Mac recognized the insignia on his fatigues. French Marine Commando. *What the hell was going on now?*

"Everyone be seated." Major Maxwell gave the order. She waited until they were all settled before she began speaking. "We've been put on alert. Command sent word this morning." She inclined her head toward Nastjia, called Nasty by her teammates, who began passing out a report to each of the men at the table.

The short, pretty man who came in last cast his eyes over her, assessing Nasty in the way bolder men did when they spot a beautiful woman. Nasty's eyes narrowed and she glared at him. Mac knew that look. It was her, "Fuck off," look. It usually worked too. Although beautiful, Moreno was fierce, and most men were smart enough to back away when confronted with that look. The pretty man's lips spread into a half smile, one that clearly indicated he was not very smart. Mac caught his eye, scowled at him, and with a quick negative shake of his head, let the man know Moreno was off limits.

The pretty man's eyebrow shot up, and with one last long look at Nastjia, he turned to the report in front of him, but a sly smirk rested on his lips. Mac glared a moment longer concluding he would need to keep his eye on short straw.

He redirected his attention to the report Nasty placed in his outstretched hand. The top line grabbed his attention. CARTEL WAR IN QUINTANA ROO.

Mac glanced sideways at Eastwood. The man rubbed the reddish whiskers growing out on his jaw, one dark-blond eyebrow raised. Further down the table, Ben whistled, and Jackson drummed his fingers on the table deep in thought. Next to Jackson, Matt chewed a toothpick as he read through the rest of the report. Mac didn't bother. He knew the major would be explaining all the bullet points before Matt made it to the bottom of the page. He turned his attention to his commander.

Major Maxwell looked around the table and then addressed the team. "Before we get to the point of this meeting, I would like to introduce three new additions to the unit," she said, sending a pointed look at Eastwood and Mac, "courtesy of your time in Kiev."

Mac cursed under his breath. Eastwood squirmed in his chair. While on mission in Ukraine, they caught the attention of a Mossad agent. That agent, Ari Solomon, reported back to his superiors in Israel revealing evidence of the rumored American Spec Ops team called PATCH-COM. From that point on, their allies insisted on being included. General P.K. Davidson was not happy about this at all and only gave in to a trial run. One soldier per ally to see how it went.

Syd continued on, ignoring their discomfort. "From the Israeli Defense Forces, we have Captain Moses Zigman, from the 414th Nesher Field Intelligence Battalion, Gaza sector."

Zigman offered the briefest of nods, a hint of hostility in his amber eyes. His demeanor broadcast the fact he did not wish to be there. Observing the man's state of annoyance, Mac recalled the Mossad agent, Ari Solomon. Once he verified their existence, the agent was both disdainful

of PATCH-COM and oddly intrigued. Amused even. He
wondered if Solomon was responsible for choosing Zigman
as the first guinea pig for Israel's participation in the experimental unit. Whatever the case, as far as he was concerned,
the feeling was mutual. They did not need anyone forced
into their midst who didn't want to be there. It made for
an unreliable teammate, one who could get themselves, and
anyone else on the team, killed. He didn't like it. Nope.

"Next to him are Flight Lieutenant Carter Ridgewood
III of the British Royal Air Force and Petty Officer First
Class Lucien Montcourt, Marine Commando, France."
Ridgewood smiled and nodded to everyone around the
table, the blue-eyed boy through and through, while Montcourt smirked assessing each man around him until his
brown eyes came to rest on Nastjia. For her, the smirk disappeared, replaced by a devilish grin.

He regarded her with pure male appreciation, murmur-
ing, "Tout le plaisir était pour moi.." (The pleasure is mine.)

Nastjia's eyes narrowed and her nostrils flared, a sign Mac
was more than familiar with from his teammate. She was
beyond annoyed and ready to spew venom. He smacked the
table startling everyone and, sending another threatening
glare in the Frenchman's direction, spoke to his major.

"So, what's the situation?" He knew his question would
come off as insubordinate to outsiders, but Mac's history
with the major put him on solid ground to rein in the po-

tentially volatile situation being stirred up by the pretty-boy new edition. He would deal with that one later, explain the boundaries and instill a little respect in the horny little toad. Right now, he just wanted to know what, exactly, was going on south of the border.

Major Maxwell noted the exchange between Mac, Montcourt, and Moreno with a slight shake of her head. "I expect everyone to make formal introductions at the conclusion of this meeting, but right now, we need to get down to brass tacks. Last night, there was an assassination attempt on Ignacio Zamora known to our intelligence community as El tejón. El tejón is the heir apparent to El Chapo, the former head of the Sinaloa cartel. The assassin was Oscar Fernandez-Ochoa, the Capo of the Colima cartel, a branch of Sinaloa. As you might suspect, this has caused a war to breakout between the two factions."

Ben whistled out loud. Matt and Jackson waited, confusion on their faces. Art adjusted his chair, leaning onto the table. Eastwood asked the million-dollar question.

"What does that have to do with us? Cartels fight among themselves all the time. They're not our jurisdiction."

Syd nodded. "You're right, but in this case, American civilians are involved." She picked up a remote from the desk, hit the button, and a screen slid down behind her. Stepping off to one side, she pointed again, and a map came up on screen. "This is the state of Quintana Roo. You're all familiar with it as a popular tourist destination. Playa del Carmen, Cancun, and Tulum. Here," she pointed with a laser, "is the Blue Parrot Paradiso Hotel. It's a smaller establishment than the large resorts around it. Think Howard Johnson's. It has no gated grounds, no real security, and it is, unfortunately, ground zero for this family feud between El tejón and Fernandez-Ochoa. Our intelligence shows the Colima assassin and his men are holed up here holding the civilians at the hotel hostage after the failed attempt on El tejón. Neither Colima nor Sinaloa has any respect for human life. Statistics prove this time and again. The State Department is trying to negotiate their release, but this is only buying us a bit of time. We have a small window of opportunity to get inside and get these people out. There are six hostages that we're aware of," she said. "A couple from California with two children, a boy and a girl, both under the age of ten, one male British citizen, and one female American citizen. The other guests were Mexican nationals and released already. Fernandez-Ochoa kept the high-value hostages."

Mac raised his hand.

"Yes, Sergeant?" she acknowledged.

"How do we know this?"

Major Maxwell faced the group, placing her hands on the table. "Because we have a man on the inside."

"Another hostage?" Eastwood asked.

"No, Sergeant," she said, "an undercover agent...in the Sinaloa cartel."

"Well, fuck me," Mac mumbled.

"You mentioned a window of opportunity, ma'am?" Jackson redirected to the point of it all.

Maxwell nodded. "Tonight. Maclean," she said, addressing Mac, "You'll take lead on this one. This is your wheelhouse as ranking Airborne specialist."

Mac nodded, a sudden sick feeling in his gut. He ignored it for the time being.

Maxwell continued, "You have one hour, gentlemen and lady. I expect you back here, packed, and ready to move out. This is a rescue operation. Mission parameters are clear from both the State Department and the CIA. Don't get involved in the cartel feud. Locate and extract the hostages. You'll be flown to SOCOM, MacDill Air Force Base. From there, taken by helo down into Quintana Roo. As soon as you hit the point of entry, our inside man will lead you to the Blue Parrot Paradiso. He'll have the specs. They've already been sent by Intelligence and he has been briefed. He will not be coming in with you. Can't blow his cover no matter what happens, got it?"

Everyone nodded, taking it all in.

"Good. After you secure the hostages, you'll lead them to the predesignated extraction point where you'll all be airlifted out. That's it. Nothing fancy. Don't fuck it up." She looked at the three new additions. "This is your audition, gentlemen. Don't screw the pooch."

Carter Ridgewood nodded. "Yes, ma'am."

Moses offered a grudging nod, and Lucien smirked, mischief in his brown eyes. "Oui, Major."

Maxwell looked from Zigman to Montcourt, her expression wary. She wasn't a fan of expanding PATCH-COM to their allies, not so soon in the development of the unit. But it wasn't her call. General P.K. Davidson had been backed into a corner by Israel, Britain, and France once their secret was leaked thanks to Mossad. Australia and Canada also wanted in but had yet to submit candidates. She knew that was coming soon, however. She just hoped they weren't troublemakers like Zigman and Montcourt. She could smell the insubordination on them. Ridgewood would be no problem, and for that, at least, she was thankful. But the other two... She shook her head. "Be back in one hour, packed and jacked. Dismissed."

CHAPTER 2

This wasn't how it was supposed to be, she thought. Connie Wheeler sat on the floor in the corner of the Blue Parrot Paradiso conference room. The red carpet with gold diamond pattern smelled moldy. On her left, a couple from California sat hugging their two children tight; a boy with dark brown curls and serious eyes who looked to be about eight and a girl with the same curls, but longer hanging down her back in ponytails. Her eyes reflected fear and she appeared to be no more than five. The parents were in their late twenties. The husband was tall with the beginnings of love handles around his waist and the wife, the one with curly dark hair, was short and slightly sunburned. She held onto the boy and the little girl clung to her daddy.

On her right, an older man with a close-cropped white beard and silver hair sat leaning forward putting his body between her, the couple with children, and the three men standing in the middle of the room carrying semi-automatic weapons. He had a charming British accent and a fatherly demeanor. From the moment they were all hauled out of their bedrooms at gunpoint, he took on the role of protector, but Connie was sure if push came to shove, he wouldn't be much protection at all, not from bullets. And they had no weapons of their own. Worse, they had no idea what was going on. Her Spanish was lacking but the older gentleman, who introduced himself as Nigel, said he spoke the language fluently. Then, he swore her to secrecy saying it would be best if the men with guns didn't know anyone in their group understood what they were saying.

"It might be our only advantage in getting out of this in one piece," he whispered. Connie noticed he didn't say, "getting out of this *alive*," and she was grateful. She was already scared out of her wits.

Having her hotel room door kicked in while she slept, being dragged out of bed with the barrel of a gun pointed at her head was not what she expected when she came to Playa del Carmen. In fact, it was why she ran away. Ten years of marriage to an abuser was more than enough years wasted. She lost nearly all of her twenties and two years into her thirties to Kevin and his rage. After the concussion and broken arm, she knew she had to break away before she was discharged from the hospital. If she'd gone home with him this time, she was sure he was going to kill her. With help from a Phoenix police detective, an attorney, and her big sister Jo, arrangements were made.

Assault and domestic battery charges were filed. Kevin was arrested and jailed, but the detective warned her that since he had no previous convictions, due in large part to her own reluctance all those years to file any charges, that her husband would probably make bail and the court would slap a restraining order on him which would do nothing at all to protect her. While he was locked away for five days, a feat accomplished with the cooperation of the court, Connie filed for divorce and made her sister Jo her legal proxy to handle the paperwork. Jo, along with a police escort, entered Connie's home, packed her bags and a few boxes of personal items her sister requested, and put those along with Connie's car into storage. She left everything else behind, wanting nothing to remind her of the dark years with that man.

Happy that her sister was finally leaving her abuser, Jo planned to return to Salt Lake City, Utah, but only after she put Connie on an airplane. After a quick visit to the storage unit for her suitcase and travel clothes, they made their way to the airport.

"Go," Jo told her. "Go find yourself on a beach. Eat some good food. Recuperate. He won't be able to find you, and after this, he'll never be able to hurt you again. When you're ready, I'll be here. Love you, sister," she said, embracing Connie.

Tears welled in her eyes as she recalled their goodbye, waving to her big sister one last time before stepping onto a plane heading south of the border to Playa del Carmen, Mexico. It wasn't a grand vacation at a luxury resort, but the Blue Parrot Paradiso was affordable. Especially since she planned on remaining there for at least six months. Connie figured that would be long enough for the divorce to go through and for Kevin to give up searching for her. She knew during that time he would be on the warpath.

The first two months were pleasant. She explored as much as she was able with the cast on her right arm, the one broken when she'd used it as a shield to deflect the punches and kicks raining down on her that terrible night. It was due to come off in two days.

With help from the hotel manager, Mr. Felipe Suarez, she made an appointment with a doctor for a checkup and to get the hot, itchy cast removed. It had already been eight weeks since the bone was broken. She was looking forward to being able to swim in the warm ocean rather than just dipping her toes, but now, a new nightmare robbed her once again of her peace, of her sanity. And no one was coming to her rescue. Panic hit in a wave, and like so many times before, she stilled, turning inward, her mind going to another place. She stayed that way throughout what was left of the night and most of the day. Nigel tried to pull her out of her trance when the armed men brought in water and some food from the kitchen, but her mind kept retreating back into its safe place leaving her locked inside her own hell.

⌘

Mac stared at the pictures on the screen of his burner phone. They were passport photos of the hostages obtained from the Blue Parrot Paradiso's computer system. He wondered how the CIA's inside informant managed that trick without blowing his cover, but it was not his business. Rescuing these innocent civilians was. A couple, the Davises, were pictured. Brad and Debbie, both age thirty-three. They looked like brother and sister, but then, married couples often resembled each other. Both had dark hair and eyes. So did their children, Aaron and Emily. The fact that children were caught up in this deadly feud between cartel factions made Mac's blood boil. Especially when he looked at the face of the little girl with her big brown eyes and dark curly hair. Something inside him twitched, something he buried deep down a long time ago.

He quickly swiped over to the next picture, a British citizen name Nigel Perry. Old Nigel was in his sixties and according to his passport, traveled extensively. Stamps for

Switzerland, Sweden, Germany, France, and New York, USA littered his port of entry section. But it was the last image that caught his attention. Connie Wheeler. He wasn't sure why, but something in her eyes drew him in. Brown, her passport indicated, but they were big, with long lashes, and...haunted. Her oval face was framed by long curls. The lighting in the picture was terrible making it appear she had a bruise under her left eye. According to her information, she was thirty-two years of age, lived in Phoenix, Arizona, and if the dates were correct, this was her first passport, her first travel outside of the United States. There was no one else checked in with her. He wondered what she was doing down in Playa del Carmen all alone.

He looked around at his teammates. Each was strapped into their seats inside the CH 47F Chinook transport chopper. It took four and a half hours to fly from Nevada to MacDill in Tampa. From there, they immediately boarded the chopper. In all, their travel time would take nearly eight hours getting them into Playa around sundown. From that point, they were to meet up with the CIA's contact, some character called Griz. No other identifying info was offered, only that he would make himself known at the coordinates provided. But that was neither here nor there. The immediate focus for Mac was the jump. The team had completed several training jumps over the past many months, and each time, he fought back a panic attack. Something about the jump triggered his PTSD and sent him back into sessions with Dr. Delaney.

The anti-anxiety drug she prescribed helped, but that was training. This was no practice run. This was full-on back in the saddle. He wiped his brow and focused on the face on the screen. His own fear did not matter right now. Connie Wheeler's did, and that's what he grabbed onto like a drowning man to a life raft. She needed him. They all did. Mac swallowed and mumbled to himself, "Suck it up, Maclean." He reached into his pocket and pulled out the small bottle of anti-anxiety medication. Twisting off the lid, he shook a pill out into his hand and popped it into his mouth, swallowing.

"Thirty minutes out," the crew chief yelled over the roar of the blades.

Taking a deep breath, Mac glanced over at Eastwood, Art, Jackson, Ben, Matt, and finally, Nasty. They all looked to him as team leader for this mission. He would not let them down.

CHAPTER 3

A voice in the distance yelled. It grew louder and yet she couldn't make out the words. Connie Wheeler blinked, and then gasped as a hand grabbed her roughly by the arm pulling her to her feet.

"Whatsa matter with you, Puta? Don't you hear me talking to you, eh?"

A hand smacked her across the face.

Chaos erupted in the conference room as Nigel and the other man from their group jumped to their feet, both shouting at the thug who hit the American woman.

"That's enough!" They yelled. The tall, dark-haired man next to Nigel glared at the heavily armed abuser while Nigel placed a restraining hand on his arm.

Connie looked from Nigel and the children's father to the thug in front of her still gripping her arm. He'd dropped the semi-automatic machine gun slung over his shoulder when he reached out to smack her. It hung at his side, swinging back and forth. She hated guns. It was a hate born of fear and having one so close to her person made her cringe. When he once again pointed it at Nigel and the others in her group, including the children who were now crying, she snapped.

"Stop it! Stop it right now! Don't you dare point that gun at those children!" She covered her ears as she screamed.

The man gave her an incredulous look, one dark eyebrow raised. "Then you do what I say, Pendeja. Comprendé? Don't make me ask twice!"

His English was heavily accented, but she understood. "I got it," she bit out, her dark eyes narrowing. She was getting tired of being the victim. Glancing at the terrified children, she decided then that there was no way she would let her fear become the instrument used to hurt them.

"What do you want?" she asked.

He pulled her away from the group. "You gonna do something for me," he said.

Five armed men aimed their guns at the other hostages who began to protest. She looked at them attempting to offer some reassurance. She mouthed, "It's okay," then turned her attention back to the one acting as leader. He had a hard look about him. Not just rough but mean. The skin on his face was scarred by acne leaving a craggy surface only partially covered by a mustache. His black hair was slicked back, and he wore a well-tailored dark suit. Still, there was no hiding who he really was. A thug. A criminal. His men were not as well-dressed but also not garbed as bums. Their clothing indicated a certain amount of wealth. Slacks, not jeans. Dress shoes, Polo shirts, and expensive watches and jewelry. These were not common criminals. If she had to guess, she'd say drug dealers. Successful ones at that. But something had gone wrong and now they were holding her and the others hostage.

"What do you want me to do?" Asking only made the queasiness in her stomach worse.

He led her to the bar on the far side of the conference room. "You're going to take a message to El tejón's Capo."

The name meant nothing to her. "Who?"

He looked at her like she was stupid. "His name is Felix Aguirre. You will deliver this envelope to him." He held up a letter sealed inside an envelope with the Blue Parrot Paradiso logo on the outside. Hotel stationary.

"How am I supposed to do that? I mean, where is this person?" Connie didn't like the idea of walking out of this room. Staying in it, however, was not appealing either, but leaving everyone else behind while she walked into an unknown situation seemed worse.

The man in the suit snorted his frustration. "One of my men will drive you. It has been arranged."

Shit! Connie looked at Nigel and the couple now huddled once again protectively around their children. She swallowed and looked the man in the eye. "I don't know who you are or what your problem is, but if you hurt these people, I'm going to make sure you suffer for it." Her words amused him.

He smiled. "I am Oscar Fernandez-Ochoa, and if you do as I say, they will live. If you fail…" he let his words trail off as his smiled faded, his finger tapping the gun. "Comprendé?"

She knew she had no choice. "What do I do then?" Her voice, so strong a moment before, was now more subdued. The one thing Connie understood well was how to diffuse an abuser. If you complied, they usually de-escalated their anger. Usually.

"Good," he said. "Muy Bueno. You take this," he said, placing the envelope into her hands, "and go. Ramon will take you."

One of the five men in the conference room came up behind her. He was bigger and meaner looking than Fernandez-Ochoa. She eyed him and then allowed herself one last look at the other hostages. She hoped it wouldn't be the last time she saw them.

"Vamos," Oscar said to her. To his man he added, "Make sure she gives it to Aguirre. No one else."

"Sí, Jefé."

Ramon took her arm and steered her out of the conference room into the twilight. The air was heavy with humidity, but a brisk breeze countered what would otherwise be a stifling heat. It was a night in which she would be happy to be out, maybe having dinner, but the reality of the situation ruined that thought. So did the sight that greeted her eyes when they left the hotel. The Paradiso was surrounded by armed men, all dressed in a similar manner as her escort. She counted more than forty men just going out to the black SUV. Fernandez-Ochoa had an army locking down the hotel. This was bad. Very bad. Worse, she was being forced into the vehicle wearing only her gray pajama pants and striped tank top. She didn't even have on a pair shoes. And she needed to pee. Her fear ramped up and her mind threatened to retreat again, but she knew she couldn't allow it. She needed to stay sharp, look for clues, for a chance to get away. She didn't know if she was brave enough to run, but the alternative was sure death. For her and for the others.

She gripped the envelope Fernandez-Ochoa gave her wondering what was written inside. It was sealed offering no chance to look. It was most likely written in Spanish anyhow. She sat in the backseat while Ramon went around to the driver's side getting in. Connie was positioned behind the passenger's seat where Ramon could easily keep an eye on her in the rearview mirror. As they drove away from the Blue Parrot Paradiso, the last rays of the sun disappeared behind the horizon leaving the sky a dark slate gray, growing darker by the minute. That same darkness might be her saving grace, if a chance to run presented itself. Her only thought was to find a way to get help. She sat straight and remained alert.

"Courage, Connie," she muttered. "You're going to get out of this alive." Part of her wasn't convinced. She lived for years with that same thought but somehow, she'd managed to jump from the frying pan into the fire. What she really wanted to know was why this Oscar character needed her to deliver his letter. Why couldn't he just send his man? A sick feeling coiled like a serpent in her belly. Of course. If El tejón didn't like the message, he'd kill the messenger. And she was the messenger.

❧❧❧❧ ❧❧❧❧

The Chinook hovered over the drop zone. Having refueled several times midair the flight crew was now prepared to bunker down in a safe place until called. That is, if Mac would just jump.

He stared out the door into the night sky, wind whipping his face. Mac took a deep breath and motioned for the team to take position on the ledge and prepare for a group launch. They lined up, seated on the edge, feet dangling.

The pilot relayed to the Dropmaster who, in turn, gave the thumbs up to the Jumpmaster. The safety belt was removed, and the JM placed his hand on Eastwood's back. He jumped. Nastjia was next followed by Ben, Art, Matt and Jackson jumping as a unit per their retraining, and two of the three new probationary members, Moses Zigman and Lucien Montcourt. For safety, Carter Ridgewood would stay with the flight crew, his own injury still a liability on foot, but he could pilot any aircraft if necessary. Finally, the hand landed on Mac's back. He worried that his trauma would cripple him, that his mind would shut down, but the muscle memory kicked in and he leaned forward pushing off the ledge.

As the wind embraced him and the ripcord deployed his chute, he breathed a sigh of relief. Years of training took over and Mac successfully completed the jump. Of course, he gave some credit to the anti-anxiety medication prescribed by Dr. Delaney.

Once the team removed their harnesses and stashed the now discarded chutes beneath a mass of low-hanging palms, they pulled out ta map, getting situated.

"We're here," said Nasty, pointing at a section on the map. "Cenote Hondo is just south. We need to travel north to Highway 307 at this mile marker," she pointed again. This is where we're to meet our contact. It's seventeen minutes to the Blue Parrot Paradiso by car from there."

Mac nodded. He looked at their group. "Everyone okay," he asked.

Eastwood glanced at Jackson, then Art, Ben, Matt, and the two new additions, Moses and Lucien. Everyone was intact and eager to get this show on the road. "We're good," he said.

"Holiday, you bring up the rear," said Mac. "Harry," he said, addressing Sgt. Harold Tyler, aka Eastwood, "you're with me. Jackson and Matt, pair up. Nastjia, you and Diaz together," he said, eyeing Art, and then, "Zigman and Montcourt, you're the final links in the chain before Holiday," he said, nodding towards Ben.

Each acknowledged their assigned roles.

"Good. Move out." Mac took the lead, Eastwood at his back. The group moved as a single unit steadily through the small open field where they parachuted in. Once they reached the tree line, they turned north along the dark road that led into and out of Cenote Hondo. Wearing black and olive camo, faces painted black with an oil stick, they were virtually impossible to see should anyone happen to drive onto the road. The rising moon offered the only light by which to see. Within eight minutes, they reached 307. Mac gave a hand signal and dropped low. The team stopped, hunkering down behind him.

In the tall shrubs they waited, watching the road. There were no cars this far out at night. They didn't have long to wait. A vehicle approached slowing down and coming to a stop after pulling off the road. It was a military transport truck with a canvas-covered bed, more than enough room for a team of nine and six more if all went well. Someone got out, walking around to the passenger side, and lighting a cigarette.

Mac observed, still hidden in the underbrush with the team, silent as the grave.

The tall, dark figure took a drag and blew the smoke out slowly. Another couple of puffs and the cigarette was flicked to the ground and crushed under a booted heel.

"You guys gonna sit there in the damned trees all night or are you coming?" a deep voice asked. He coughed and spit. "We ain't got all night. Time's wasting."

Mac's eyebrow shot up and he pursed his lips. Standing, he signaled for the team to rise. He walked out of the shadows into the moonlight and approached. The man came into view. He had dark hair and eyes with a salt and pepper goatee. Irritation flashed across his face.

"I take it you're Griz," said Mac. "Sergeant Maclean," he said, offering his hand.

The tall man gave Mac the once-over, then threw a quick glance at the team. He shook his head. "Never woulda believed it if I hadn't seen it with my own two eyes." He ignored Mac's hand and moved to the rear of the truck throwing the canvas flap open. "I don't have a fancy wheelchair lift." He patted the bed of the truck. "Just gotta haul yourselves in."

Mac's eyes narrowed. "Fucking prick," he mumbled. To his team, he issued the order, "Load up."

One by one they climbed into the back of the truck. As they passed, Eastwood, Art, Nasty, and Ben all flipped Griz off.

The man chuckled, unfazed. When they were settled on the bench seats, he pulled the flap back into place. "I'll get you as close as I can. Word is the Colima soldiers have locked the hotel down. Last I knew, all the hostages were inside."

Mac poked his head out. "And how many cartel guns?" he asked, referring to Fernandez-Ochoa's men.

"Close to fifty. And that's just the Colimas. Sinaloa men are positioned as well. Think you can handle that?" Griz asked.

Eastwood leaned out next to Mac. "We can handle it, fucker. Just drive. Time's 'a-wasting,' remember?" he said, throwing the man's words back at him.

Griz grinned. "You're some feisty sonsofbitches, I'll give you that. Never knew broke dicks had so much spunk." He looked past Eastwood at Nastjia Moreno. "And a freaking woman on the team too. Ain't that a bitch."

Nasty glared at him. "What rock did they find you under?" she asked.

"Ha!" Griz's eyes twinkled. "Might be some hope for you," he said, then threw the flap back down, getting serious. "Now stay put until we stop, and I give the all-clear."

Griz got in the driver's seat and cranked the ignition. As he pulled back onto the road performing a U-turn, Mac blew out a breath, his nostrils flaring. "Don't like him. CIA can fuck itself after this."

Nasty agreed. "When did we ever think otherwise?"

CHAPTER 4

The truck rolled to a stop. Mac and the team waited in silence, ready to move. The flap opened and Griz poked his head in.

"We're here." He backed out of the way to let them out.

One by one they dropped down. Jackson and Moses had the most difficult time of it. Jackson's brace was manageable beneath his pants, but his range of motion would always be limited on the right leg. Moses Zigman's left leg remained braced from above the knee down. Bullet-riddled in one of many battles along the Gaza strip, infection had set in and it was touch and go for while as to whether it would need to be amputated. He pulled through, but the damage was great, and he was only six months into rehab. Sheer stubbornness was the fuel that drove him on despite the pain.

Griz eyed the men taking mental notes of their injuries. He was particularly impressed with the prosthetic arm belonging to the blond called Rogers. It moved independently as if directed by the man's thoughts. He had heard of such but had never seen the technology in person. Rogers gripped his SOPMOD M4 rifle with the same confidence as if he had both his natural arms. The injuries of some of the others were not as obvious. He couldn't see the prosthetics on the one Sgt. Maclean called Eastwood nor could he see any such on the tough-talking woman, but he did detect slight limps from both. However, he had yet to figure out the remaining three, Diaz, the Frenchman, or the mission leader, Maclean. And there was no time for questions. It was Griz who took the risk contacting his handler inside the CIA the moment he'd heard about the hostages.

Once alerted, Washington D.C. took action to protect their own. Griz hacked into the hotel's mainframe while conducting surveillance on the Blue Parrot Paradiso—the surveillance being a direct order from Felix Aguirre. The Capo wanted to know how many Colima soldiers were on site and where. He especially wanted to know the location within the hotel where Oscar Fernandez-Ochoa had holed up after the attempted assassination on El tejón went south. Griz mapped the number and location of each man from a safe distance using the tech at his fingertips. Tapping into the hotel's security cameras from his laptop, he found Fernandez-Ochoa in a conference room on the southwest side of the hotel. He had also pulled up the guest list gleaning the passport information of each person checked in.

The president of Mexico arranged for the release of all Mexican citizens on the list in exchange for not interfering in the cartel's business. Five blocks all the way around the perimeter were evacuated by local police. But Colima would not release the high-value hostages, five Americans and one British national. They were bargaining chips and Fernandez-Ochoa was desperate. Having them in his possession kept even Sinaloa at bay. They all knew the rules of engagement. America and Britain would not interfere in cartel business unless the cartels harmed one of their own. In that event, there was no law that would prevent both America and Britain from sending in troops to retaliate and no one wanted to spark that war.

So, Griz forwarded the information to the CIA who brought D.C. into the loop. A negotiator contacted Fernandez-Ochoa via the hotel's main phone line. The story they presented about how they discovered the hostages was easy enough. A hostage already released video, posted it to social media that went viral. It wasn't true, but it was plausible. To add credence to the tale, Griz patched some of the security camera footage he'd hacked into a short video and uploaded it to Twitter through a VPN. As intended, it made the rounds quickly garnering thousands of views within a few hours.

And now here they were. Washington D.C. and the CIA collaborating with the military sent in a rescue team, and it was the darndest thing he had ever seen. He still couldn't believe it. Had only heard rumors about a unit of broken soldiers or broke dicks as they were known. Fucking PATCH-COM. Patch 'em up and send 'em back out.

Griz pulled a device out of his back pocket. He hit a button and the screen lit up. "This is where we are," he said, pointing at a vector on the electronic map. "You travel to the end of this block and turn right. One block over is the hotel. This puts you on the southeast end. There are only about seven men guarding that section right now. See?" He indicated the red dots moving slowly back and forth caught by the drone camera he controlled.

Mac studied the image. "And the hostages?"

Griz tapped the screen and it rotated. "Here. In the southwest corner conference room. That area is heavily guarded, but if you go up the fire escape ladder at this point of entry, you can avoid those men and attack from within."

Mac considered all the scenarios. He'd been in tighter situations than this, but not with civilian lives on the line. The quicker and quieter they got in, the better.

"How many men inside?"

Griz switched the screen to a live camera. "Looks like five men plus Fernandez-Ochoa. And he's here right now," he pointed. "Just outside of the conference room with these two soldiers. That leaves three inside with the hostages. There's a bar at the far end with a storage room behind this refrigerator unit. I checked the hotel plans. This duct system runs from the second-floor housekeeping quarters over this storage unit. It's a small space where they store the liquor. Now, you can get maybe two men in there, but the only way out besides the main door leading to Fernandez-Ochoa is through to this second smaller conference room. There are two windows and they face the southeast side. I don't know if they have the ability to open or are fixed. I suspect fixed."

Mac looked at Eastwood.

"Probably storm windows, the kind designed to withstand hurricane-force winds. Wouldn't be able to break them out." Eastwood speculated out loud.

"Why can't we take them out the same way we go in?" Nastjia asked.

Griz cocked his head. "You're all trained for this. The civilians aren't. I guess you could, but it's not the best-case scenario. What if one of them is too big to fit into the duct? What if the kids cry or make too much noise?"

Mac stopped him. "It may be the only way considering the alternative, which, if we can't open a window would mean shooting our way out the front. Can't do that."

Ben Holiday agreed. "We get two men in to take out the three guards inside the room. One of us stays in the duct to pull up the kids fast and get them out. The other two are responsible for getting the adults up and through."

Moses nodded. "No time to worry about windows when we don't know that situation. We extract the same way we come in. But it has to be quiet. No guns."

Lucien pulled a wicked hunting knife from a sheath at his hip. "No problem."

Mac eyed the knife and quirked an eyebrow at the Frenchman. "Then you're with me, Short Straw."

"It's Lucien..." he began.

"It's what I say it is," said Mac. "We're the two most able-bodied." He looked at Nastjia. "Moreno, you'll be behind us in that duct. Kids are calmer with a woman, so you'll be responsible for getting them out." She nodded. "Eastwood, Zigman, and Rogers, you're at our back. Diaz, Hicks," he said, looking at Art and Jackson, "I want you on the perimeter. You're our cover. Anyone comes around from the southwest side, take 'em down."

Griz watched as Maclean outlined the plan in short order. Satisfied they had it under control, he handed the truck keys over to the Sergeant. "It's your show now. I have to get back before I'm missed. Vaya con Dios, gentlemen," he said, and then threw a cheeky glance and mocking bow at Nastjia, "and lady." He gave a two-finger salute and took off in the opposite direction.

Montcourt glared at his back. Eastwood and Holiday chuckled.

Mac handed Nastjia the keys. "Just in case," he said.

Taking the keys, she slid them into her pocket.

Mac signaled for Lucien to get behind him. In stack formation and keeping to the dark paths, they moved quickly down the block and hooked right. Another block over and they arrived at the southeast parking lot of the Blue Parrot Paradiso. Dropping down behind a line of parked cars, Mac took in the scene.

There were still seven men walking the back lot, submachine guns in hand. Two were smoking by an old pickup truck. Three paced a line back and forth between the rows of cars. One leaned on the trunk of a vintage Chevrolet, and the seventh wandered out past the last parked car nearest to where they hid. That one stepped off the curb between two of the cars, unzipped his pants, and pissed a stream into the gutter.

Mac locked eyes with Eastwood and, keeping low, came around the back of the car to the sidewalk, behind the man. An arm snaked out clamping a hand over the thug's mouth. Mac's free hand shoved a Bowie knife into his neck. As the thug's body crumpled, Eastwood caught him, dragging him around and rolling the dead man beneath the car. One down, six to go.

They moved in closer. Mac had Diaz and Hicks take up their locations to cover the southeast perimeter.

"What we really need is a distraction," Mac whispered.

Moses Zigman watched the Colima soldiers pacing. "Didn't Griz say Sinaloa had men watching?"

Mac nodded. "He did. What are you thinking?"

Moses looked around behind them. "I haven't seen any hint of them out here on this end. Have you?"

Mac shook his head. "Nope, haven't. That's odd."

Ben and Eastwood exchanged a look. "The major said he was the CIA's inside man. Inside Sinaloa, right? He looks the part. Plus, he's an asshole, but that's beside the point. If he is and he somehow left this quadrant wide open, we're the only ones who know this. That means those Colima ya-hoos think their enemy is out here where we are." Eastwood let his thoughts run.

"But there's some sort of negotiation going on, so no one is making a move," said Ben.

"Yet," Moses added.

"We need to draw them out, but not in a way that will have them sounding the alarm."

Ben bit his lip, thinking. Eastwood and Mac sighed in frustration.

Zigman shook his head. "How do you Americans get anything done? You have the bait. Use it!" He looked at Natsjia.

Nasty's head whipped around. "What? You want me to just go out there and show them my tits?"

Lucien spoke up. "Non! You will not put her in that kind of danger."

She looked at the Frenchman. "I can handle myself, Montcourt."

Zigman continued. "She won't be in danger. She has all of us. Just make yourself known. Lure them away from the parking lot. We can ambush them here, out of earshot of the rest of their army. It's the quickest solution because any moment now they're going to notice they're one short."

Mac looked at Nastjia. "You comfortable with that?"

She nodded. "But I'm not showing my tits."

"No one asked you to," said Zigman. "Just throw the come-hither looks. You're attractive enough. They'll come."

"But you'll have to lose the battle gear," Ben said, eyeing her rifle and vest.

"Shit," she mumbled, and then began divesting her protective gear.

"I don't like this," Montcourt said. "Cherie, you don't have to do this."

Nasty eyed him. "Listen up, Lucky," she said, ignoring the flash of irritation in his eyes at the moniker and the snickers from Eastwood and Ben, "I am a Navy SEAL, the first female Navy SEAL at that. That means I had to be tougher than any man to make it into that all-boys club. Got it? I can filet you like a fucking fish, so cut the misogynistic bullshit." She pulled a bandana and a small canteen from her bag. Soaking the cloth, she scrubbed her face clean of the oil stick. When she finished, she handed her gear to Holiday who set it down on the ground beside him. "You assholes just be ready because I am not in the mood to be molested by cartel thugs tonight."

Nasty moved down the line of cars keeping low. When she cleared the last parked car along the curb, she stood, arched her back, and began a slow saunter towards the hotel. The two men having a smoke noticed her first.

"Hola, Chica," the taller one smiled.

The three men patrolling stopped and eyed her warily. They approached quickly, two from the left and one on the right.

Nastjia noted she could easily have dropped all three and then killed the other two sucking tobacco smoke into their lungs before they could say "boo" but that left the sixth man still leaning against the trunk of the vintage Chevy. He had not moved, but rather, eyed her with suspicion. That

made him smarter than his buddies and far more dangerous. She needed to draw them all out.

"Hola," she said sweetly. Looking at their guns, she allowed her eyes to pop wide. "Wow, ¿hay alguna celebridad
en el hotel esta noche? ¿Quién es?" (*Wow, is there a celebrity
at the hotel tonight? Who is it?"*) Nasty played the innocent.

The first of the patrolling men who reached her side
gave her the once over. Sensing no threat, he grinned. "No,
morena, but you can't be her tonight," he said, replying in
Spanish.

She pouted.

The two on a smoke break chuckled and joined Nastjia
and the guard. "Carlos, you're no fun. She's just what we
need to pass the time."

Carlos shook his head. "Some other time, bebita," he
said, trying to shoo Nasty away. The smokers came to her
side and linked her arms in theirs.

"See? She's friendly. You're friendly, aren't you pretty
one?" The shorter of the two smokers, who had a round
face and a paunch for a belly gave her butt a squeeze.

Inside, she cringed. Outwardly, she smiled, then cast a
sly look at the man leaning on the Chevy. "I am, but what
about that one? He looks like an irritated bull."

The smokers laughed. The round-faced one coughed and
pointed. "That's because his wife never gives him any—"

The bull stood, pointing his rifle at the round-faced man. "El Jefe will kill us all. You know shit is serious right now, Juanito, so get your fat fingers off the whore's ass and send her on her way. We don't have time for this shit!"

Nastjia changed tactics. The angry bull wouldn't be drawn away by flirtation. He was wound too tight. She needed to break his control.

A slow smile spread across her lips. "Well, no wonder his old bitch of a wife won't give him any. He's too mean and ugly."

Juanito dropped his hand from her ass and backed up. Carlos threw her a look that said, *'Run now!'*

She ignored them both and turned to the taller smoker. The man wore a black leather vest over a white t-shirt paired with jeans and black biker boots. He was younger than Juanito and Carlos, not bad looking. She stood on tip-toes allowing her breasts to brush his chest. "Want to show the sourpuss how a real man pleases a woman?" She said it just loud enough to reach the bull's ears.

She could almost see his eyes turn red before he charged. Anticipating the attack, she pivoted throwing black vest backwards into the charging bull's path and ran toward the street. The bull gave chase, more pissed than before after colliding with the younger man.

"Puta, I'm going to kill you and fuck your skull!" he said, hot on her heels.

Mac kept his eyes on Nasty, but as the situation evolved, sent Montcourt and Holiday around the opposite end of the line of cars where they hid. Carefully, they moved through the rows of parked vehicles coming up behind the vintage Chevrolet. With the Colima soldiers distracted, they positioned themselves for attack. When the angry one took off after Nasty, the three patrol guards followed. The two smokers stayed behind, guns hanging loosely from straps over their shoulders. They watched their comrades chase the girl and never saw the two who came from behind, knives to their throats. As they dropped, Montcourt and Holiday pulled them between two cars and dropping low, took off after the patrol guards.

As soon as Nastjia ran through two of the parked cars along the curb, the bull followed, three patrol guards at his back.

Montcourt, sprinting like an Olympian, dove onto the back of the last patrol guard, his hunting knife cutting off the man's scream before it could leave his mouth. Holiday tackled the next one rolling like a gator and snapping the man's neck.

Mac launched himself at the bull throwing a punch to the side of the man's head. The bull staggered but did not fall. He turned in time to see his backup taken down by a large man with a reddish beard who punched his comrade repeatedly before plunging a knife into the guard's chest with a violent twist.

The bull shook off the hit and turned his attention to Mac. That was his mistake. The moment his back was turned, Nastjia jumped on it and in a move worthy of Bruce Lee, pulled him down, swinging her body completely around and locking her legs around the bull's head. With one quick flex, she broke his neck.

Mac stood over her, hands on hips. "Coulda just let me finish him off, you know," he said.

Panting, she glanced at her team leader. "Sorry. But he did call me a whore."

Mac grunted, extending his hand to help her up. "Fair enough." He looked at Eastwood who was pulling the body of the patrol guard between the cars. "Six more down." The rest of the team assembled, and Mac looked from one to the next. "Not much time left. Let's get our people out."

CHAPTER 5

Connie peeked at the massive mansion before her. Ramon put the SUV in park and was about to get out when several armed men stopped him. He threw his hands up and froze. A man stepped forward and looked into the backseat. He had a thin mustache and a large nose. He chewed a toothpick casually as he eyed her.

"You," he said, pointing at Connie, "come." He glared at the driver. "You stay," he said, patting Ramon on the head, "like a good boy." He opened the back door and waited for Connie to exit the vehicle. Throwing a last look at his men, the man added, "If he moves, shoot him."

Terrified, she walked carefully over the concrete of the driveway onto the flagstone leading up to the massive oak double doors of the house. They were thick and heavy, crafted to last. The man she followed walked fast and when she lagged behind, looked down at her feet noticing they were bare. An eyebrow quirked, but he was unmoved.

"Ondelé!"

Not wanting to anger him, Connie caught up. He pushed open the door and stepped inside. Cool marble tiles greeted her bare feet as did a large, arched hallway. Art lined the walls on either side. Expensive art. No doubt purchased with blood money.

The hall led to a cavernous living room that was connected to an open terrace. She could see an infinity pool beyond that looked out over the Caribbean Sea. Several women were at the pool, swimming, lounging poolside, in bikinis, drinks in hand. Upbeat music played from a sound system built into the outdoor bar. A man stood looking out, his back to the room. He wore a gold silk robe, one arm in a sling. He was tall, but a taller man stood to his right, and a shorter man to his left. The shorter one was well-dressed in a suit and tie. The taller one wore a black vest and jeans.

The man with the thin mustache stopped behind them. He waited quietly for the group to acknowledge his presence. Connie stood in the background shifting back and forth, her hands clasped in front of her body.

Finally, the man in the gold robe turned, and noticing them, asked, "And who is this?"

Thin mustache answered, "A message from Fernandez-Ochoa."

The other two men next to the one in the gold robe turned their attention toward her. The suit looked mean with close-set beady eyes and a pointed chin. The tall one, however, was far more intimidating. His dark brown hair was shot through with silver matching his goatee. He was big enough to snap her in two, but it was the look in his eyes that bothered her most. It was anger, and she didn't know why he would be angry at her. She'd never seen him before.

"A message?" The gold robe eyed her, and then, "What's wrong with her? Why is she doing that?"

Thin mustache noted her dancing movements. He shrugged. "Don't know."

Gold robe addressed her directly. "What are you doing?"

Connie could see he was talking to her, but she had no idea what he said. "I don't speak Spanish. Sorry."

Gold robe's eyes narrowed in irritation. He glanced back at the tall one. "Vicenté, you speak English. Ask this bitch what her problema is."

The tall one stepped closer. "He wants to know what's your problem. Why are you doing that," he pointed at her tippy-toe dance.

Connie's faced turned red. How, she wondered, does one tell drug lords who might kill her at any moment she needed to pee?

"Well?" Vicenté asked.

She looked down, collected herself, and then in an act braver than she felt at the moment, one that might prove the dumbest thing she'd ever done, said, "I was yanked from my bed in the middle of the night last night by men with guns. I've been kept in another room all day at gunpoint by those same men, and quite frankly, I have to pee!"

The one called Vicenté looked like he swallowed a live bird whole. He opened his mouth once, and then closed it again before turning to the gold robed man. He relayed what she said in Spanish.

The man in the robe eyed her, then burst out laughing. Connie had no idea what to think even as the thin mustached man laughed along with his boss. The tall one and the short one did not join in. The gold-robed man's laughter died as suddenly as it began.

"She has a message for me?"

Thin mustache looked at Connie. "The message, what is it?"

Unclenching her hands, she produced the letter. "I don't know. He sent this."

Thin mustached snatched it from her hand startling Connie who pulled her hand back and wrapped her arms around her body. He handed it to his boss.

The gold-robed one looked at the envelope, now crinkled from being gripped in her hand, and said, "Take her to the restroom." He looked down again at her feet. "And get her some shoes. We are not animals."

Thin mustache gripped her arm painfully yanking her away, but the tall one stepped in, his menacing glare enough to make the other man back away.

"I'll take her." He looked at Connie and stepped aside, indicating which way she should go.

She stepped carefully around him not knowing what was coming next until Vicenté leaned down and whispered, "Relax. I'm just taking you to the lady's room. And I'll find you some shoes."

Kindness was the last thing she expected, and it confused her more. She looked up at him. "Is he going to kill me?"

Vicenté eyed the woman in her gray striped pajama top and solid gray bottoms. "I don't know yet."

They turned right into another long, arched hall. Midway down, he stopped in front of a door. "You can take care of business in here. I'll find you some shoes. What size?"

Connie looked at her bare toes. "Seven and a half medium."

He nodded and waited until she stepped inside the bathroom. The door clicked and she realized she'd been locked inside. Who had locks on the outside of bathroom doors? Panic grew, but her bladder intervened.

If nothing else, she thought, *I won't piss myself when they kill me*. She sat down quickly, feeling a moment of instant relief followed by a nagging fear that she would not get out of this alive. She eyed the cast on her arm. It might be the only weapon she had, but what good would conking one of them on the head do when there was an army of men, with guns, waiting to blow her to bits? She thought of her sister Jo, and the friends she left behind. Ten years she'd been trapped in an abusive marriage, one she finally got out of only to run headlong into a more terrifying situation. *What did I do wrong, God? Why is this happening?*

Tears slid down her cheeks and she wiped them away before cleaning up. Standing before the sink, she looked at herself in the mirror. She was a fright. Her hair sat atop her head in a messy bun. The pajamas were wrinkled, and she needed a bath. More than anything, she wanted to run away from everything and everyone and never look back, but that's what got her into this mess in the first place. She splashed water on her face and patted it dry with a towel. Sniffing back tears, she waited for the tall one to return with a pair of shoes. Shoes. Why would they give her shoes if they were just going to kill her? It was such a crazy thought, but her mind grasped onto it like a drowning person reaching for a life raft. The fact that she was being given a pair of shoes seemed like a sliver of hope, a sliver that said maybe, just maybe, she would survive the day. It was all she had, and she clung to it. *Please, God, please send help.*

Mac moved forward through the air duct making slow but sure progress. Behind him, Lucien Montcourt stayed on his heels. After scaling the fire escape, his team entered the premises by way of a small window using a glass cutter to quietly create a hole through which to unlock it. Once inside, they located the housekeeping closet Griz pointed out on the hotel's blueprint. With Jackson 'Junkyard' Hicks and Art Diaz strategically situated outside covering the southeast side of the hotel parking lot, Mac and Montcourt located the duct, removed the vent cover, and climbed inside. Eastwood guarded the small room from the hall with Moses Zigman on one end of the hall and Matt Rogers on point at the other end. Nastjia Moreno followed Montcourt inside the duct. It would be her job to assist the children inside the duct and lead them out.

It was dark inside the duct, but with the night goggles it was clear as day. They made good time on elbows and knees. In seven minutes, they were at the vent over the storage closet behind the conference room bar.

Mac stopped and looked through the grate. Faint light filtered in through a crack in the door leading out. There was no one inside the storage room and it was quiet. That did not work to their advantage. Without noise from the other room Mac had no idea if the hostages were still inside, and the lack of sound meant they had to be extremely careful, as silent as the grave, removing the vent cover and dropping down. That left no room for mistakes.

With steady pressure, Mac popped the grate open. It swung open on its hinges, but he guided the cover with his hand to prevent it from banging the wall. The ceiling was only nine feet from the floor and there was a table directly below about five to six feet down. An easy drop. Mac crawled forward over the opening until he was able to touch the table, Montcourt holding his feet. Once through, he stood on the table helping lift Montcourt out until his feet were clear of the duct. One at a time, they dropped down from the table to the floor.

Nastjia peeked her head out and gave Mac the thumbs up, waiting. He removed his night goggles and pointed toward the partially open door leading out. She nodded. Mac looked at Montcourt who already had his 9mm Glock in hand, silencer attached. Mac mounted the suppressor to his own handgun and patted the sheath at his left hip. The hunting knife was snug within, but checking it was akin to the automatic adjustment all men performed when grabbing their junk through their pants. Just reassuring it was all still there.

The door was ajar just enough for Mac to peek out. He dropped low and cocked his head looking around. At first, all he could see was the backside of the bar. After a minute, the visible upper body of a guard walked past, the strap of a machine gun over his shoulder. He wore a blue shirt with a collar. Fancy for a thug. Listening, Mac could hear the gunman's muted footsteps across the carpet. His were the only feet moving as far as he could tell, but that didn't mean he was the only cartel soldier inside the conference room.

Easing out and disturbing the door as little as possible, he moved into the small space behind the bar allowing Montcourt to come out behind him. The bar was about twelve feet in length with two exits, one at the far end, and one three feet from the storage room door. The one closest to them was a cut-through. Inching closer, Mac and Montcourt looked around the edge of the bar out into the conference room. It was a large room, and they could see the entire area from their vantage point. The guard with the blue shirt walked the perimeter of the room. He held the submachine gun, but his posture was relaxed. He was not showing any urgency or tension. A second guard sat in a straight-back chair smoking a cigarette. Ten feet away, the hostages sat against the wall.

Mac recognized them by their passport photos. The couple with two young children leaned against the wall, their kids laying across their laps. The husband held his daughter, and the wife had her arms wrapped around her son. Although they appeared at first glance to be napping, their eyes would pop open, look around anxiously, and close again. Except for the little girl who did appear to be deeply asleep. The older British man, Nigel, watched the guard in the blue shirt making his rounds from beneath half-closed lids. Mac glanced left and right. Where was the American woman?

Unable to locate her, a feeling of dread snaked through him. Had they already killed her?

The guard in the blue shirt walked back toward the bar. Nigel, watching him, caught sight of movement and suddenly, locked eyes with Mac.

Mac placed a finger over his lips.

Nigel's expression froze but he nudged the American man next to him who came to. There was a silent exchange between them and then the American's eyes made a casual sweep of the room before landing briefly on the two men barely perceptible behind the passthrough of the bar. He let his eyes continue on but reached out to take his wife's hand giving it a squeeze.

Blue shirt was almost to the bar, and if he decided to walk behind it, would discover more than whiskey and wine.

Nigel sat up. "Any possibility you might let an old man use the bathroom?" he asked, speaking Spanish.

Blue shirt turned around. The second guard tossed his cigarette onto the carpet and crushed it with his boot. He looked annoyed but stood.

"Come, Viejo," he said, "you can have that corner all to yourself." He pointed at the far corner nearest the window.

Nigel got up slowly, his eyes quickly looking at Mac. To the other hostages he said, "Anyone else need to go? Kids?"

The guard sighed. Blue shirt shrugged.

The American couple got up and took the children to the far corner. Nigel followed. The guards waited; their backs turned.

Mac and Montcourt moved fast, guns drawn. Mac dropped the guard wearing the blue shirt with a head shot and Montcourt took down the second guard with two through the back of his skull.

The American parents covered the children's eyes and shielded their bodies with their own. Nigel ducked low.

Mac eyed the door leading out of the conference room, his M4 aimed and ready. Montcourt moved to the side of the door and listened. He looked at Mac and gave a thumbs up. No one heard a thing. No one was coming in...yet.

Moving fast, Mac approached the hostages. "I'm Sgt. Maclean and I'm here to get you out and back to America. Stay quiet, stay low, and do what I say, okay?"

The adults nodded. Nigel whispered, "Thank God.

Mac looked at the kids, the boy first, and then the little girl. Her trusting brown eyes tugged at memories he couldn't afford to indulge. His spirit screamed, *Save her!* Out loud, he said, "Don't you be afraid. It's going to be alright. My friend is waiting for you all in the storage room. We're going to take a fun trip through a tunnel. Can you do that for me?"

The boy nodded, and the little girl sucked her thumb, but her big brown eyes looked at Mac with awe. His heart palpitated as the memories of another pair of trusting brown eyes passed through his mind's eye on a loop. Chills ran down his spine and his vision narrowed momentarily. He shook himself and, taking a deep, even breath, concentrated on the task at hand.

"Okay," he said, "but you have to be very, very quiet, okay?" He gestured for them to go into the storage room. Mac eyed Nigel, speaking low. "Where is the other hostage? The American woman?"

Nigel shook his head. "We don't know. They took her out."

"Who?"

Nigel pointed toward the closed door leading out of the conference room. "The one called El Jefe."

Mac bit his lip. "How long ago?"

"About an hour now. He said he wanted her to deliver a message."

Shit, Mac thought. That could mean a lot of things. The worst-case scenario being they killed her but why would Fernandez-Ochoa do that? The Americans, all, were valuable leverage. No, he wouldn't kill her, but he would use her as a shield. That meant he sent her in to deliver a message to El tejón. This complicated things. There was no way of knowing where she was sent. And El tejón might not be as concerned about killing an American hostage. Maxwell explicitly told them not to fuck things up. It didn't get any more fucked than failing to rescue all the hostages.

Right now, however, they needed to get this group out. He ushered them inside the small storage room, the American couple's children first. The little girl didn't want to leave her father's arms, but Nastjia cajoled the little one into allowing her to take her into the duct, promising daddy and mommy would be right behind her. The boy went next, then the mother, and last, the father. Getting Nigel up into the air duct was tougher. The old man was out of shape and it was a tight squeeze, but Mac threw his shoulder into it and the British gentleman's feet finally disappeared inside the dark duct.

Mac signaled to Montcourt who came in behind him. Together, they re-entered the vent moving toward the housekeeping closet where Eastwood and the men waited.

So far, so good.

Mac took lead once again in the hallway leading out to the fire escape. Rogers and Zigman were last out and down the ladder, watching their six. The parking lot was clear as they made their way through the row of cars.

They were almost to the street when Mac caught sight of headlights slowing down and turning into the lot. He motioned for everyone to get down.

"Moreno," he said, summoning Nastjia over. "Get them to the truck. If I'm not there in fifteen minutes, get them all to rendezvous. You have the coordinates."

"What? No! We all go back together," she said.

"We're one hostage short, Nastjia. That's unacceptable. And that was an order." Mac eyed her, his words stern.

She opened her mouth, then closed it. Not at all happy, she rounded the hostages up. "Follow me. Stay low. Keep quiet. We'll be moving fast." She looked at the American couple. "Carry the kids if you have to, but don't stop."

She led the way. Mac sent Montcourt, Zigman, Jackson, and Rogers with her.

"You're with me, Harry," he said, throwing a quick glance at Eastwood. To his right, Art Diaz waited on orders. "Diaz, you too. Head up that row. Get in position to cover the driver. We don't know who's in that vehicle or how many, but we need to find out where they took the other hostage. Harry, take the rear. I'll cover the passenger side. Move out."

CHAPTER 6

The drive back to the Blue Parrot Paradiso was far more stressful than her earlier journey. It was almost better not knowing what she was walking into than knowing now what was to come.

After she was escorted back into the main living room wearing the sandals given to her by the tall man called Vicenté, sandals a half size too big, she was put through a frightening interrogation by the man in the gold robe. Using Vicenté as his translator, he introduced himself formally.

She froze, terrified.

The name Ignacio Zamora was not unknown to her. She'd heard it more than enough times on the news, always in connection to drug trafficking and brutal killings throughout Mexico. If she hadn't already, she was sure she would have pissed herself. Connie knew her situation was bad, but until that moment, she hadn't considered exactly how dire. *How the hell did I walk into this?*

Zamora was known to his enemies as the badger for the viciousness in which he murdered his enemies. Beheadings, full-body dismemberment, gutting people like fish, all made the headlines. Her terror escalated to a level where she feared she might shut down completely, and that would be a costly mistake.

She tried to answer all of his questions. How many men did Fernandez-Ochoa have with him? Where were they situated? How many other hostages and what nationalities were they? He asked about guns, but she didn't know anything about firearms. Frustrated by that, he ordered several of his guards inside to show her their guns and asked her if that's what she saw. She could only nod yes or no, unsure if the answers were right or wrong. A machine gun was a machine gun to her. Same with handguns.

When he was satisfied, he told her she would return to the hotel with his answer to the message from Fernandez-Ochoa. Then he had Vicenté and the guard with the thin mustache take her back out to the waiting SUV. As she climbed into the backseat, she screamed. The driver, Ramon, was slumped over the steering wheel, his brains splattered across the dash and front seat. Thin mustache man laughed at her reaction, but Vicenté betrayed a hint of sympathy. He gave her shoulder a comforting squeeze.

Thin mustache pushed Ramon over and began climbing into the driver's seat. Immediately, Vicenté yanked him back by his collar.

"I'll drive her," he said. Thin mustache argued, but Vicenté stopped him cold, getting into his face, a deadly glint in his eyes. "You already fucked this up, pendejo. That attempt on Zamora's life happened on your watch," he added, his tone low and menacing, "and don't think he's forgotten." The man's thin mustache twitched, wanting to say something, but he backed off, hands up in surrender.

Vicenté got in and pulled away from the house. Looking into the rearview, he told her, "Buckle up. Shit's about to hit the fan."

Connie swallowed down the bile threatening to rise. The stench of blood inside the car, the sight of bits of bone and chunks of flesh was making her sick. Vicenté caught her eye in the rearview and rolled down the windows in the backseat.

"See if there's a towel or a blanket back there behind you."

Connie leaned her face out of the window and took a deep, cleansing breath. Then, she turned, rummaging around in the spacious trunk area of the SUV. There was a red-checked blanket. She righted herself and handed it up to Vicenté who slowed briefly, shaking it out one-handed over the dead men shoved into the front passenger's seat.

"That's about as good as I can do for now," he said, looking over his shoulder. He noted the paleness of her face and the fixed look in her eyes. She was in shock. He shook his head and turned his attention back to the road. "It'll be over soon."

Connie nodded. Silently, she wondered at the consideration this man was showing her. He looked every bit as frightening as the rest of the cartel thugs, but he showed her kindness and just now, consideration. She'd lived ten years with a man who'd blown hot and cold. This was nothing new, but this thug had yet to be cruel. But he did just say it would all be over soon. Did this mean she would be part of the message sent back to Fernandez-Ochoa? Would she, too, soon be just bits of splattered blood and bone?

God knew she wasn't a religious person, not anymore, but with no one left to help, she bowed her head to pray. *Please, Lord, it's me, Connie Wheeler. I know I stopped believing in you a while back. I still don't know why you let Kevin keep beating me, why you left me bruised, broken, and all alone despite all the times I asked for your help. I don't know what I did to deserve it then, and I don't know why this is happening now, but please, I'm not a bad person. I'm not! Please, God, please help me.*

Tears rolled down her cheeks and she turned her face to the wind breathing in the warm night air of the Mexican Riviera. What should have been the first steps toward her freedom now revealed themselves to be the last march to her death.

※↠↠↠ ↞↞↞※

Mac eyed the SUV rolling to a stop in the parking lot. His M4 trained on the passenger side, he waited. The window in the backseat was down and a face poked out, taking a deep breath. He recognized the face. It was the American woman! He glanced at Eastwood catching his eye and gave the signal to hold position. Eastwood passed it on to Diaz on the other side. They stayed hidden, watching.

She appeared to be having a conversation with the driver. Her eyes went wide, and then she opened the back door looking around like a scared rabbit.

Mac heard a voice say, "Run to the street, one block down, and then one block over to the right. Get to the nearest consulate office." His ears perked. He knew that voice.

The woman took a few hesitant steps away from the vehicle and turned. "But why? Why are you letting me go?"

"Because they don't know if Zamora kept you or killed you, and Zamora doesn't need you anymore. This is your chance to get away."

"But what about you?" she asked.

"I have a message to deliver. That part can't be avoided." He pointed at the dead, blanketed lump in the seat next to him.

Mac had heard enough. He stepped out; gun pointed down. "I'll take her from here."

Connie jumped, and stumbled back.

From inside the SUV, the voice said, "Don't be afraid. He's a friendly. U.S. military sent here to rescue you and your fellow hostages. Go with him. Now. Hurry."

Mac moved to her side gently taking her arm. He noticed the cast and wondered as he did when he first saw her passport photo what had happened to her. Why was she here alone in the first place? But there was no time for speculation. "He's right. We need to go now." Mac looked inside the vehicle noticing the barely covered body and the mess. "Come with us. Nothing good can come from this, Griz."

"Griz? I thought your name was Vicenté?" Connie asked, completely confused.

Griz offered a self-deprecating smile. "It's actually Vincent. Vincent Torres. That's classified information so keep it to yourself. And people back home call me Griz, ma'am."

His Spanish accent was noticeably gone. Connie gasped. "You're American?"

"Yes, ma'am."

Her mouth hung agape. "But, but..." her eyes grew wide. "You're undercover!" she whispered. "But you can't go in there. They'll kill you."

Griz smiled. "They'll try. And I'm not going in. I'm just dropping this dead weight off. Don't you worry. It ain't my first rodeo. Go with Sergeant Maclean. He'll get you out." To Mac, he added, "Did you get the others?"

"We did. But one was missing," said Mac, looking at Connie Wheeler.

Griz reached over the dead body and shook Mac's hand. "Get her out of here, amigo. Fast."

Mac nodded. "I got her. Good luck."

Griz drove off heading around to the front of the hotel.

Mac gave Connie's arm a gentle tug. "Ms. Wheeler, we need to go." He signaled to Eastwood and Diaz who joined them.

She looked at Mac for the first time. Really looked at him. "Where are the others?"

"Already on their way to rendezvous with the rest of the team. That's why we need to hurry." He led the way to the street, and then told her, "Stay behind me. Sergeants Tyler and Diaz have our backs. We're going to be moving fast."

She swallowed and bobbed her head acknowledging his words. She'd prayed for help and here he was. Connie's eyes roamed over Sergeant Maclean. His head was shaved. He had a nice shaped head and a rugged jawline. But his eyes were what held her attention. Hazel with dark lashes. In all, he had a dangerous look, like a Jason Statham character, but like those characters, she sensed the good in him. As they ran in single file across the street and down the block, he reached back to touch her arm and make sure he wasn't getting too far ahead for her to keep up. It was reassuring. The two large men behind her, dressed in black and dark olive camo and armed to the teeth, also made her feel safe for the first time in the last twenty-four hours.

The problem now was...she was going home, for surely that's where they would take her. As they turned a corner hustling down another block, she wondered if maybe they could drop her off somewhere else. Somewhere where there weren't drug dealers and angry, abusive soon-to-be-ex-husbands. She made a mental note to ask...as soon as they were safely away.

CHAPTER 7

S hots fired in the distance. The sound of tires peeling out was followed by more gunfire. Mac listened as he ran. They were only two blocks away from the Blue Parrot Paradiso, and by now, Fernandez-Ochoa knew his hostages were gone, and he no longer had any leverage. The fuse had been lit by the dead body Griz delivered—El tejón's answer to whatever deal Colima was trying to work out with Sinaloa, a last-ditch effort pleading to not be brutally massacred after attempting to kill the heir apparent of one of the biggest cartels in Mexico. Zamora's answer was a 'fuck you' to Oscar Fernandez-Ochoa. It was the first volley in what would now be a vicious war between Sinaloa and Colima. Anyone caught in the crossfire would be executed.

They reached the open lot. The truck and the rest of the team were already gone. *Shit!* Mac looked around.

"We need a car," he said.

Eastwood agreed, and he and Diaz assessed the vehicles parked nearby.

"What about that one," Connie asked, pointing at a blue Ford Fusion sedan.

Art eyed it utilizing the tech built into his eye prosthetic. A Marine sniper was no good without two good eyes, and when he'd lost one from a roadside truck bomb, his commanding officer recommended him to General Henning, a close tie inside the Joint Chiefs of Staff to Army General P.K. Davidson, the man responsible for PATCH-COM. "No alarm system."

Eastwood made his way to the driver's side window, and with one quick slam from the butt of his rifle, broke the glass. He reached inside opening the door and swept the glass off the seat. Getting in, he cracked open the dash and hotwired the ignition. Diaz slid into the front passenger seat, and Mac helped Connie into the back, sliding in beside her.

Mac pulled his GPS out of his vest pocket and used it to navigate their way to the location where a Chinook helicopter waited to get them out. That is, if they were still there.

The fifteen-minute ride felt longer, and when they arrived, the truck was parked in the tall grass, but the chopper was gone.

"Fuck!" Eastwood banged his hands on the steering wheel. Art Diaz shook his head. In the backseat, Mac rubbed his jaw and mentally switched gears.

"We'll need to get to the American Embassy in Mexico City."

Art looked over his shoulder. "What about the local consulate?"

Mac shook his head. "It's not protected," he grunted. "The Marine Security Guards only protect the building and the vital information, not the people. And their ain't enough of them even for that. Too dangerous to even try with the cartels declaring all-out war. We need to take back roads out of here and get to the embassy as fast as we can."

"Point me in the right direction, Sergeant," said Eastwood. "I'll get us there. Hell, if I don't, my wife will kill me."

Art chuckled. "She can be formidable," he said, thinking about Eastwood's wife. She was the founder of Win-Runner, the prosthetic company now contracted with the military exclusively for PATCH-COM. A bio-tech prodigy, Joely Winter invented the weaponized, technologically advanced prosthetics fitted to each soldier brought into the top-secret unit based at Camp Lazarus, a base hidden deep within the infamous Area 51 in Nevada's Groom Lake.

Eastwood grinned. "It's what I love most about her."

"Get back onto the main highway, head southeast, but turn north here," he pointed. "It's a side road that skirts around the main strip of Playa."

Connie looked at Mac. "How long will that take?"

Mac locked eyes with the woman. "If we stayed on the main roads, about nineteen hours, but..."

"But what?"

"We need to avoid the toll roads. We don't know yet if anyone will be looking for you, and even if they don't, this cartel war is going to cause hell all over the country. They'll be looking for anyone suspicious. That's us. So, going the slower routes, it may add another day. Maybe two."

Connie bit her lip and looked down at the pajamas she wore since the night before. Two more days, maybe three, and she wasn't even wearing a bra! Crossing her arms over her chest, she leaned back and stared out the window.

Her discomfort wasn't lost on Mac. She probably hadn't eaten anything all day and yet she had not once complained. There was an inner strength in this woman that impressed him. Mac reached for his carry kit; a cross-body bag all Spec Ops carried. Unzipping the bag, he pulled out an extra black t-shirt, a granola bar, and a small bottled water. It wasn't much, but it was the best he could manage at the moment. Quietly, he handed the items over.

Surprised, Connie took the bundle from the Sergeant, thankful for the kind gesture. She opened her lips to express

SECOND CHANCE SOLDIER   85

her gratitude, but the words were choked off by the unexpected lump in her throat. She sniffed, blinking rapidly to quell the sudden flood of tears. It had been a long time since she last cried, and longer still since she was on the receiving end of kindness. First Vicenté, no, that's not right. Griz. He said people back home call him Griz. He'd stepped in to protect her from El tejón, had given her shoes when her feet were bare, and then put himself in danger to save her from what might otherwise have been a horrific death at the hands of Oscar Fernandez-Ochoa. And then there was Sergeant Maclean, who, by his own words, stayed behind at the hotel to rescue her because, "one was missing." And now, without having said a word he was once again saving her from an attack of modesty, and extreme thirst and hunger.

She clutched her bounty to her chest and turned her head away, eyes shut tight. She just needed a moment.

In the front seat, Art and Eastwood shared a look but said nothing. Eastwood glanced in the rearview mirror and caught sight of Mac, his expression uncomfortable as he reached out awkwardly touching her shoulder in an attempt to soothe.

Connie felt the warmth of the Sergeant's hand seep into her skin. He gave her a reassuring squeeze and then removed the hand while clearing his throat.

"Harry," he said, "make the best time you can on these back roads. In the morning, we'll find a hotel, get some rest, and then reassess."

"Roger that," said Eastwood.

CHAPTER 8

B y sunrise, they arrived at the coastal village of Paraiso in Tobasco, Mexico. They were all tired having remained awake throughout the night. Mac located a small hotel a few blocks from the Caribbean Sea with two rooms available. Connie could barely keep her eyes open as the one called Art signed them in and retrieved their room keys. She couldn't wait to take a bath and climb into a bed no matter how run down the hotel appeared.

Sergeant Maclean unlocked her door and stood aside allowing her to enter. She walked in and turned to close and lock it but ran straight into the sergeant instead.

"Ow!" she said, backing up and rubbing her forehead. She accidentally banged it into his shoulder.

"Sorry," he said.

"What are you doing, Sgt. Maclean?"

"Just Mac is fine," he muttered, "and I'm bunking with you." He dropped the bag holding his weapons onto the floor next to the first of two twin beds. He turned and looked at her inquiringly, "unless you'd rather share with Harry or Art?"

Connie sputtered, "I don't want to bunk with any of you."

Mac sighed, hands on hips. "No choice right now. My job is to protect you and I can't do that from across the hall."

"But no one is coming for me," she said. "Vince...Griz explained it. Oscar Fernandez-Ochoa doesn't know if El tejón kept me or killed me and, well, that one let me go so he didn't have any use for me. No one cares where I am. No one is looking for me." She stopped herself from saying *anymore*. There may very well be one more person looking for her. Her husband.

Mac watched the expression in her eyes shift from confident to a sudden look of alarm, but she covered it quickly. Still, the wobble in her tone revealed her uncertainty. She was keeping something from him.

"I care," he said. "I came looking. Now, you want the shower first?" He pointed at the bathroom.

Connie's mouth opened and closed. Mac didn't say a lot, but what he did say confounded her. He was blunt, intimidating, and acted like his word was law. She was sure that as a soldier he was used to men following his orders, but she wasn't one of his men. And she didn't appreciate not having any say in roommates. Then those last words sank in. He said he cared and that he'd come looking for her. What in the world did that mean? Some broad statement of the U.S. government? Well, of course, she chided herself. He didn't know her so how could he personally care? No, he was just saying what needed to be said and that was that. But it bothered her.

"I'll shower first."

Mac nodded, sitting on the side of the bed.

Connie hesitated, looking around the room, and then looking down at her clothes. She still wore the gray silky pajamas but with Mac's black t-shirt over the tank top. It was all she had. And the drug dealer sandals. She wondered absently which of the women she'd seen lounging around El tejón's pool had been the owner of the half-size too big shoes. She felt grimy and tired and all she wanted at the moment was a shower, and clean clothes, and sleep. She'd have to settle for the shower and sleep because clean clothes seemed to be out of the question. Feeling defeated, she walked into the bathroom and closed the door.

Mac stared at the bathroom door. Connie Wheeler didn't speak a word, but her face said a great deal. Getting up, he left the room. In the hall, he knocked on Harry and Art's door.

Eastwood answered. "What do you need?"

Mac eyed him. "Keep an eye on her. I'll be back."

With a brief nod, Eastwood came out and leaned up against the wall next to Ms. Wheeler's door. Mac made his way down the hall and out into the bright morning light.

The hot spray from the rusty shower head made everything better. Connie shampooed her long brown hair as best she could with one hand, keeping her casted arm out of the way, and then conditioned it. She was thankful that despite how rundown the place looked, they did provide free shampoo and conditioner. Washing away the grime of the last few days lifted her morale. She glanced at her dirty clothes on the bathroom floor. The t-shirt was the cleanest of the items, but her underwear, pajama pants, and matching tank top were in bad shape. She bent down and scooped them up, and using the soap, attempted to wash them. Another ridiculously hard task with the cast. After wringing them out, she hung them over the shower rod hoping they would dry quickly. In the meantime, she figured she could wear the t-shirt to sleep. It landed mid-thigh and she would be under the covers, her modesty protected.

With no comb or brush, she ran her fingers through her tresses before winding her hair up and securing it atop her head with the dark brown scrunchy. It would do for now. Finally, she opened the mini-mouthwash bottle and swished it around and over her tongue. Feeling much more herself, she left the bathroom.

Mac was gone. Having no idea where he went or how long he would be out, she ran across the room and quickly climbed into the twin bed next to the far wall. The sheets were cool and the pillow soft. It was quiet except for the hum of the air conditioner. She thought about the last few days and wondered how in the world she managed to get through it all. Mistreated and beaten, constantly on edge. And she'd seen a dead man, his brains blown out. It was a nightmare, but she survived.

Now she was surrounded by soldiers hell-bent on protecting her and getting her back home. She should be thankful, and she was, but home was not safe. Her eyelids drooped and her last thought was a mental reminder: Ask Sergeant Maclean if he could drop her off somewhere else. Maybe Mexico City. Or Texas. Anywhere but Phoenix.

Her arm itched and she stuck her fingers into the cast to relieve the irritation. Also, she thought, her mind going fuzzy, see about getting this cast off.

CHAPTER 9

Mac returned in an hour dropping off a couple plates of food to Eastwood who smiled as he inhaled the aromas.

"Nice, boss. Tacos?" he asked.

"Enchiladas," Mac said. "Any problems?"

"Nope. All is quiet. I'm guessing she's sound asleep."

Mac nodded. "Good. You two eat and get some rest. We'll head out after sundown."

Eastwood took the food into his room, closing the door. Mac shifted the bags he held and unlocked the door, entering the room cautiously. It was cool, dark, and quiet inside. A soft snore greeted his ears. Connie Wheeler was tucked in tight and laying on her side facing the wall. He locked the door and set the bags down on the small two-seater table. He'd picked up some easy to reheat street tacos with all the fixings for both of them and bottled water. He ate his portion and then slipped into the bathroom for a quick shower and change of clothing.

When he came back out, he set a bag next to her bed and then climbed into his own, laying back atop the covers trying to get comfortable. Something hard poked his side. Sitting back up, he slid his sidearm under the pillow. Once he was resettled, Mac glanced over at the sleeping woman. Her hair had come loose and was spread out over the pillow. He could smell her subtle scent on the air, the hotel shampoo, no doubt. It had been a long time since he was alone in a hotel room, or any room for that matter, with a beautiful woman. And she was beautiful, although he wasn't entirely sure she knew it. Her dark eyes framed by thick black lashes gave all her thoughts away. But sometimes, her face shut down as if trying to keep the world out.

He remembered her passport photo, how the lighting cast shadows under her eye making it appear as if she'd gone a round or two in the boxing ring. He didn't see any hint of a bruise when he found her last night, but the cast on her arm brought up questions, as did the fact that she was here all alone. He wanted to ask, but knew it was none of his business. Yet it bothered him.

The last time he worried so much about a woman was...well, more than two years ago. And that had been a waste of his time. Paula made clear that she couldn't handle him being away so much, and then she could not handle when he came home all messed up. Nothing he did pleased her, and after far too many arguments, she left. He asked her to go to counseling with him, but she refused. He begged, pleaded for a second chance, but in the end, she filed for divorce. It was months later when he discovered she had been having an affair with a coworker while he was deployed, and his homecoming threw a monkey wrench into her adultery.

Heartbroken, Mac buried the pain of her betrayal and focused instead on working through his PTSD with Dr. Delaney. Some progress was made, but there were still moments when it would get the better of him, and moments when he exploded in anger. The tools Dr. D gave him to cope with the first issue didn't help at all with the second. And since he never confided in her about his divorce, she was flummoxed when his anger spiraled out of control. Time, however, did help heal that wound. Or, at the very least, it scarred over. Mac stayed away from women after that. He simply was not ready to open the door to a new romantic relationship. So why was he even thinking about all of this now?

Glancing again at Connie Wheeler, he sighed. *Nope,* he thought. *No fraternizing with rescues. Don't even think about it, Mac!*

Closing his eyes, he drifted off into a light sleep.

It was late afternoon when Connie cracked an eyelid. Fatigue weighed her down and the thought of moving at all was not appealing, but a nagging sound pulled her from Morpheus's grip. She looked around the room, confused at first as to where she was or even the day of the week. It all came flooding back. She turned her head and saw Mac on the other twin bed. He was laying on his back, one arm over his head, and snoring like a bear.

It was the sound a person made when their body was completely exhausted. She wondered if she'd been snoring too. She hoped not. That would be embarrassing, but not nearly as embarrassing as being caught wearing only a t-shirt and no bottoms. Spurred to action, she slid out from under the covers and put her feet on the floor, trying to be as quiet as possible. Her foot hit a bag and she froze.

Mac snuffled, turned his head, and began snoring once again.

Breathing a sigh of relief, Connie looked at the bag. She had no idea where it came from, but it was sitting next to her bed. Peeking inside, she saw clothing. Women's clothing. She paused and glanced at the sleeping soldier. Had he gone shopping for her? There was a scent on the air too, one that made her stomach growl. Across the room, sitting atop the two-seater table was another bag. She recognized that type of bag. Food.

Exercising care, she picked up the bag and tip-toed to the bathroom. Closing the door, she took the time to inspect the contents within. Pulling the items out one by one, she discovered two t-shirts, one in bright pink with a tropical graphic printed on the front, and a dark blue with lighter blue crochet lace around the neck and the sleeves. Beneath the shirts were two wrap-around skirts. One matched the pink shirt, and the other was white cotton gauze with dark blue flowers. Last, she found a smaller bag containing ladies underthings; simple white nylon and lace bikini panties and two sports bras in white. A smart choice when he couldn't possibly know her bra size. Mixed in was a hairbrush, toothbrush, and what looked like a gift with purchase lotion and lip gloss kit. It was incredibly thoughtful.

Connie looked at her pajamas hanging over the shower curtain. Reaching up, she felt them. Still a bit damp. But that didn't matter now. She took her time getting dressed, enjoying the fact she actually had a choice of what to wear. After brushing out her hair, applying some lotion to her skin—a light scent of French Lavender—and dabbing on a bit of berry lip gloss, she looked at herself in the mirror. The pink t-shirt and matching pink wrap-around skirt brought a glow to her cheeks that she hadn't seen in many years. The skirt reached her ankles and flowed loosely, which helped hide the fact that the slide-on leather sandals given to her by Griz were half a size too big.

For the first time in a while, she felt human.

Rolling her pajamas in a dry towel, she placed them inside the bag and repacked her things. At least she wouldn't be showing up at the American Embassy in dirty clothes. That was a blessing. And there was food in the next room. With a smile, she exited the bathroom.

Mac was still asleep, and she had no idea if he ate yet. She set her bag down by the end of her bed and approached him. Reaching out to touch his shoulder she intended to give it a light shake.

"Sergeant Maclean," she whispered.

Mac's hand shot out grabbing her arm. He yanked her down and rolled her over until they both landed on the floor.

Connie screamed as his hand went around her throat. "Stop!"

Mac's eyes were wide open, but something was off. It was like he didn't see her. She screamed again, kicking and punching, her blows having no effect.

"Sergeant!" she squeaked out.

Mac shook his head, his eyes focusing. When he saw Connie Wheeler beneath him, his hand gripping her throat, he released her immediately jumping back and moving off the terrified woman. He leaned against the bed, panting, mortified.

Connie coughed and rolled over taking deep breaths. Her hand at her neck, assessing any damage, she slowly sat up. Behind her, Mac tried to get himself together, panicked apologies rolling off his lips.

"Jesus, fuck, I'm sorry. So sorry. So sorry." He glanced her way, his eyes wide. She sat with her back to him. "You okay? Fuck, I'm so sorry." He reached out to touch her shoulder and she jerked away. His hand dropped. "Ms. Wheeler...I'm..."

"Sorry. I know. I heard you. It was my fault. I shouldn't have touched you." Getting up, she walked to the table, keeping her back to the man, her spine stiff.

"Wasn't your fault. It's me. I'm...fucked up." That admission was hard to make. Mac got up and sat on the bed. He grabbed his duffel bag and rummaged around for his pills, taking one from the bottle and swallowing it down with a sip of water. "That's what these are for," he said, tossing the bottle back into the bag, disgusted with himself.

Connie turned, leaning on the table. "What, exactly, are they for?"

Mac sat with his head resting in his hands. "Post-traumatic stress."

PTSD. She noted the subtle shaking of his shoulders, a tell-tale sign of his distress. She could relate. She had her own issues. "You didn't know where you were for a minute did you?" She experienced that same feeling when she woke up, but it didn't make her react violently. Then again, she wasn't a soldier.

"Didn't even know it was you," he mumbled. "I really am sorry. I didn't hurt you, did I?" Mac looked at her then, his eyes raking her from head to toe, his gaze coming to rest at her neck. Shame and horror filled his eyes.

Her neck throbbed a bit, but she decided to keep that to herself. "I'm fine."

Mac stared at her for a long time. He knew when a woman said she was fine she was not fine. He stood, walking over.

Connie wanted to back up, but she was already against the table.

Reaching out, Mac lifted her hair out of the way. He inspected her neck. Gently, he touched her skin just below her ear and down under her chin. He sighed, eyes closing tight, his face a portrait painted in shades of shame and remorse.

She shivered. For a large man, he had a soft touch. She swallowed hard.

"Fuck, that's going to bruise." He looked into her eyes then, his fingers caressing where only moments before they were wrapped around her neck in a death grip. "Connie, I'm sorry. It won't happen again. I promise."

His words were ones she'd heard before. Ten years of promises never to hurt her again, and yet Kevin had broken every one of those promises. She pulled away, sliding over to break their contact.

"It's fine," she said. A rote reply. It was unfair to him, she knew, but this scenario felt like every moment of abuse she suffered in her marriage. She didn't know how to handle it any other way and moved immediately into distraction mode. This role she knew. It was easy, effortless. "So, I see you brought food."

Mac saw the walls she threw up right away as if they were built of mortar and stone. She was keeping her distance and changing the subject, but there was fear in her tone, and he hated that. In that moment, he realized this was nothing new, that she'd been a victim of violence before. He remembered the passport photo and looked again at the cast on her arm. Someone had hurt her, and now, he was one of those someones. *Fuck!*

He stepped back, giving her the distance she needed to feel safe. "I ate earlier. That's for you. Tacos and all the fixings. I can heat it up for you in the microwave."

"I'll do it." She carried the food to the small sink area containing an even smaller microwave. In minutes, her food was hot, and she sat down to eat.

Mac retreated to his bed. "What happened?" he asked, pointing at her cast.

Shrugging, Connie gave the easiest answer. "I broke my arm. The cast was supposed to come off yesterday. I had an appointment in Playa with a doctor. But that all went south."

Having broken a few bones in his military career, Mac sympathized. But he also knew she wasn't telling him the whole story. "I can remove it if you like?"

She put down her taco. "You can?"

"I've cut off a cast before. It's not hard."

Connie looked at the itchy thing. It would be nice to have it off. "Okay."

Mac was surprised she agreed. He was certain she wouldn't trust him again after nearly choking her, even if it was accidental. Hope bloomed.

"How will you do it?"

He pulled out his hunting knife. "This will cut through anything."

Her eyes popped wide.

Mac sought to reassure her immediately. "I'll be extra careful. We can go slow. Or I can get one of the men to do it if you'd rather..."

The offer to have one of the other two men take over struck her as sincere. He really was filled with remorse. "No. You do it. But let me finish my dinner first."

Mac nodded; his relief visible.

Connie took a bite and then asked, "How did you come to be diagnosed with PTSD?"

The question was not one he was comfortable answering. He didn't talk about this with anyone except Dr. Delaney, and on occasion, Major Maxwell. But he sensed a kindred soul in Connie Wheeler. He was curious about her, about who had hurt her. It would be hypocritical to want to know her story while withholding his own. Dare he open up? The last time he tried to explain, his wife left him.

He'd faced insurgents on every continent, fought horrific battles, and survived incredibly dangerous situations, but he'd never been more afraid than he was now, with this woman looking so beautiful in her pink outfit quietly regarding him over a street taco, awaiting an answer to the hardest question he'd ever been asked. Mac told himself not to even think about a possible relationship with this woman, but there could be no harm in a simple friendship, could there?

A bead of sweat trickled down his spine. Taking a deep breath, he braved the possibility of her rejection.

"It wasn't any one thing," he said. Mac sat with his hands on his knees, but as soon as he began to speak, they balled into fists. He forced them to relax and continued. "Doing what we do, we see a lot of things most people never even think about outside of movies or books. Lots of evil in this world, a lot of cruelty. Mostly, it's caused by men seeking either money or power, or both. Greed," he muttered. His mouth felt dry. He never spoke this much outside of therapy, and he always felt drained after sessions with Dr. D. "Saw something I wish I hadn't. I guess it was the tipping point. A man can only take so much. It messed me up. That's all."

Connie finished her food quietly, listening as he struggled to explain. He had avoided eye contact throughout most of his speech but glanced her way before falling silent once again. There was a wealth of uncertainty in that look, as if he expected her to run. She got up and went to sit next to him on the bed. Tentatively, she reached for his hand. He flinched but forced himself to remain still, letting her do what she wanted to do. His hand was much larger than her own, rougher too. It was strong and obviously capable, much like the man himself. He was a soldier who ran into dangerous situations to rescue people caught up in the crossfire of war. Connie looked up and caught him watching her, a combination of surprise and something else in his hazel eyes, something she didn't quite recognize. Something akin to hope.

He had the beginnings of sun wrinkles at the corners of his eyes, and a deep worry line above his right brow. His jaw was rugged, and his cheekbones high. It was a nice face in all, and she liked the shaved head. It was manly in an action-figure kind of way. She wondered if he ever smiled.

It was an odd thought. Smiling wasn't something she did often herself. There weren't many reasons to smile in the last ten years of her life, after all. At thirty-two, her existence had been virtually joyless. And then someone gave her some pretty new clothes and personal items. The thoughtfulness of the act had brought a smile to her face.

"Thank you, Mac."

His eyebrows shot up. "For what?"

She smiled, and it didn't feel forced at all. "For my clothes and things. That was the nicest thing anyone has ever..." she stopped, her smile faltering. "Anyway, thank you. I love them."

Moved by her words, Mac placed his free hand atop hers, which was still holding onto him. "I'm glad." His gaze ran over her form from head to toe. "You look..."

Connie waited, and when he didn't finish the sentence, prompted, "Yes?" The heat of his hand on hers stirred something inside, something she hadn't felt in a long, long time. Desire rolled over her body like a warm ocean wave.

"Nice," he said. Mac found himself drowning in the warmth of her big, brown eyes. They looked up at him now with trust, not fear. In that moment, he vowed that no matter what issues he had, he would never harm a hair on her beautiful head, not even by accident. That meant stepping up his therapy sessions with Dr. Delaney. It meant admitting he needed help, and not just the prescription variety. He'd focused on work and his gardening, but not on rebuilding his life. Only now did he realize how lonely he'd been.

The warm wave of desire grew hotter as Mac's eyes roamed her face and settled on her lips. She struggled to catch her breath, her lips parting as she inhaled.

He leaned closer and Connie's eyes drifted shut. Her heart raced, anticipating his kiss.

A loud knock on the door startled them both as Mac jumped to his feet, irritation contorting his face.

He opened the door. "What!"

Diaz and Eastwood stood in the hall, both shocked by Mac's abrupt greeting.

"It's almost sundown," said Eastwood, looking around Mac into the room. Connie got up moving away from the bed to the table where she began cleaning up.

Mac looked over his shoulder watching as she gathered the plate and bags and threw them into the trash can. Nothing more he could do now but prepare to leave.

"Yeah, we'll meet you at the car." He shut the door in their faces leaving them standing in the corridor, stunned.

Inside the room, Mac turned. "Connie, I—"

She cut him off. "I'm ready when you are." She retrieved her bag and stood in the middle of the room.

Mac sighed. Their moment was gone, and he didn't know if there would ever be another. Maybe he'd read it wrong, read her wrong. He'd just admitted to being fucked up beyond repair and she'd been kind. Maybe that's all there was to it. He moved past her to grab his duffel bag. Reaching under the pillow, he pulled out his sidearm and stuck it into the holster at his hip. Pulling his shirt down to cover it, he surveyed the room one last time making sure they both had everything.

"Ready," he said.

Connie walked to the door and reached for the knob, then paused. Mac nearly crashed into her. She looked over her shoulder and whispered, "You're not messed up. You just have wounds that haven't healed. You're a nice man, Mac." She opened the door and walked out leaving Mac staring at her back.

His lips twitched and a warm feeling filled his heart. Realizing he'd almost smiled, Mac regained his tight control and, tossing the room key onto the table, walked out, closing the door behind him. As he made his way down the hall, he found himself hoping...for what, he couldn't say, but if the moment arose, he promised himself he wouldn't hesitate again.

CHAPTER 10

For the second night in a row, they drove through the night taking back roads to avoid detection by local law enforcement. If anyone happened to be looking for them or a stolen vehicle, it would come in the form of corrupt police or Federales. Earlier in the day, Mac used the time he spent shopping for clothes to call Raymond Garza, an American Diplomatic Security Agent at the Embassy in Mexico City. Garza was their point of contact; the diplomat notified that U.S. Special Forces would be operating a rescue mission inside the country. He was in charge of coordinating with the host country. As a courtesy, the embassy generally notifies local FBI, but they did not appreciate U.S. forces putting boots on the ground inside Mexico and would rather not know, hence the need to avoid running into Federales.

When a mission went according to plan there was no need for the team to reach out to the DSA, but now that they were caught inside Mexico, they needed a safe exit route, and in Connie Wheeler's case, their assistance with legal travel documents. That meant getting to the embassy as quickly as possible. With the clock ticking, Diaz drove while Eastwood navigated. In the backseat, Mac sat next to Connie. As the car bounced over rough roads, her thigh brushed against his own. It was not unwelcome, but he could see it flustered her. There was a telling flush on her creamy cheeks.

He reached over and touched the cast. "We didn't get that off."

Connie glanced down and sighed. "No. That's okay. When I get back stateside, I'll take care of it."

Mac looked at the white surface. No one had signed her cast. He'd broken a bone in his foot and one in his lower arm once. Both times he wore a cast, his teammates signed them along with the friends he and Paula once shared as a couple. But no one had signed Connie's. It bothered him. Whipping out a pen, he gently lifted her casted arm.

"What are you doing?" she asked, surprised.

"Signing your cast." Mac picked his spot, the area above the inside of her wrist, and began writing.

Eastwood looked over the seat. "What're you two doing back there?"

Connie looked at the bearded man. The red in his whiskers contrasted with the dirty blond of his hair and darker eyebrows. A devilish glint lurked in his green eyes. She was sure he thoroughly enjoyed instigating mischief.

"Mac is signing my cast," she explained.

Eastwood grinned. "Well, heck, if we're giving autographs, I'm next."

His smile was infectious. "Autographs from my heroes. That seems appropriate."

Diaz chuckled. "I'll be happy to sign when it's this knucklehead's turn to drive."

Eastwood punched Diaz's shoulder. "Who you callin' knucklehead?"

Mac ignored his men focusing on the task.

Connie strained to see what he was writing, but he pulled her arm across his lap and was leaning against her shoulder. She couldn't see around his arm but did notice the muscles bulging beneath the tight t-shirt material. He really was a big man, and he smelled nice. Clean. Masculine. Her mouth went dry and she licked her lips.

From the front seat, Eastwood noticed Connie Wheeler's reaction to Mac's proximity. He poked Art in his side and threw a quick glance back at the duo in the backseat, his dark blond eyebrows wiggling once. Art's eyes widened, but he kept them on the road ahead. Somehow, he didn't think Mac would appreciate any teasing from them, and he definitely didn't want to embarrass the lady. His mother raised him better than that. But he wasn't sure about Harry, who looked like he was about to poke the bear.

"Hey, Eastwood, is there a turn coming up," Diaz asked, distracting Eastwood before he stuck his foot in his mouth.

"What? No, not for another ten miles," said Eastwood. "I told you that already. You got a hole in your memory or what?"

The distraction worked.

Connie, too, was drawn into their conversation. "I thought your name was Tyler. Didn't Mac introduce you as Sergeant Tyler?"

Eastwood turned; his arm stretching casually over the back of the seat. "It is. Harold Tyler, but my friends call me Eastwood."

Connie cocked her head. "Do all of you have nicknames?"

"Codenames," Mac mumbled, still bent over Connie's cast.

"Oh, I see. So, you all have them then. What's yours, Art?"

Eastwood answered before Diaz could. "Cyclops."

Art punched Eastwood in the ribs.

"Well that's not very nice," Connie said.

Art snorted. "No, it's not, but then, we don't get to pick our own nicknames. They're given by our teammates."

"But why Cyclops? You don't have one eye." Connie looked at Art's reflection in the rearview mirror.

Art offered a self-deprecating smile. "Actually, I do. The one on the right. I lost it in a roadside explosion. Truck bomb. This one is a prosthetic," he said, pointing at the right eye. "State of the *Art*, you might say."

Connie's jaw dropped. She leaned closer, looking in the mirror. "I can't even tell the difference." She reached over the seat and squeezed his shoulder. "I'm so sorry you lost an eye, Art. Does it affect your vision much?"

Diaz grinned. "It improved it, actually. This type of prosthetic is experimental and not available to the public. But maybe someday soon it will be."

"Then you're a pioneer. A man given the gift of second sight, so to speak." She turned her attention to Eastwood. "And why are you called Eastwood. Is that a cowboy thing?"

Eastwood nodded. "Something like that. I'm a weapons specialist. My old unit called me Dirty Harry, but out in the field, that's too much of a mouthful."

"I see. Well, it's nicer than Cyclops. I don't suppose you all could change that to something with a little more dignity?"

Mac listened to their conversation, still holding her cast in his hand. "Like what?"

Connie thought about it, her brow quirked. Finally, she smiled. "Bindu."

"What?' Eastwood asked, confused.

Mac huffed. "Third eye chakra. Don't you read?"

"Exactly," Connie exclaimed, impressed. "It's Art's third eye and it has helped him see more accurately."

Art smothered a laugh. "Not sure Indian mythology will fly in the field."

Eastwood settled back into his seat staring at Diaz. "Naw, Bindu isn't right. Doesn't fit him. Cyclops works," he nodded. "Let's stick with what works."

Silently, Art agreed, but out loud, he said, "Well, Ms. Wheeler, we tried."

"But it's not dignified," she said, slumping back into her seat.

Mac patted her arm. "We know his worth. Trust me."

Connie gave up. She realized Mac was finished writing, but now was holding her hand. She wanted to read what he wrote since he seemed to take a lot of time signing the cast, but his fingers had entwined with hers and the warmth of his hand was causing that warm ocean of desire to roll through her body again and she didn't want it to end.

To her delight, Eastwood seemed to have forgotten about signing her cast for the moment, and they drove the next few hours that way, the men squabbling now and again in the front seat, and Mac quietly stroking her fingers in the backseat. Oddly enough, it made her feel like a teenager sneaking around a bit behind mom and dad's back.

Eight hours passed mostly in silence. They arrived at the outskirts of Puebla and Connie was so flustered, she could barely stand it. Judging by his heated gaze, she guessed Mac was well aware of the state he put her in. It was after two in the morning and she was tired and hungry, but her body hummed. It was beyond unsettling.

Art pulled into a gas station off the main road.

"Time to gas up again. Anyone want anything from inside? Chips? A soda?"

Connie didn't like junk food. She looked around and saw a strip mall of shops and taverns. The shops were closed, but the taverns were still open. A food vendor served a small crowd of people in front of the closest bar. She had no idea what he was selling, but the scents coming in through the rolled-down window made her mouth water.

"What about the street vendor?" She pointed.

Eastwood stepped out, stretching his legs, and working the kinks out. The prosthetic on his left leg had begun to pinch and he desperately wanted to remove it to give his stump a little relief. He leaned on the right leg and eyed the food cart. There were a few locals lined up, but the crowd across the way was thinning out.

"What do you say, Mac? Feel like some tacos and roasted corn?"

Mac eyed the thinning crowd and shrugged.

Art smiled approvingly. "Sounds better than chips. I'll pay for the gas and get some drinks. Water? Coke?"

"Water for me, please," Connie replied.

"Make that two," said Mac.

"A big orange soda for me, bud," Eastwood added. "How many tacos do you want?"

Art held up three fingers. "I'll be back." He turned, heading inside the store.

Mac looked at Connie. "What can I get you?"

She smiled. "I'll come with you."

He looked around assessing their situation. Down the street, a squad car slowly made its way in their direction. He glanced at Eastwood.

"I see it," he said. Reaching inside, he grabbed his bag and Art's. Mac did the same pulling his duffel bag and Connie's store bag out of the backseat.

"What are you doing," she asked. "Why are we taking our bags out?"

Mac linked an arm through hers and began walking across the street blending into the crowd. Eastwood went inside the convenience store and after a quick word with Diaz, they both exited, casually merging into the crowd, and making their way to the vendor.

Confused, Connie waited for an answer. "Well?"

Mac drew her to the far side of the crowd standing around the street vendor. "Police," he said.

The authority in question drove slowly past them and then turned into the parking lot of the gas station. They continued on as if to exit and drive back down the way they came, but then the vehicle braked, red taillights flaring, and the car backed up.

Mac tugged Connie's hand. "We have to go. Now." He signaled to Eastwood and Diaz. "Stay behind us twenty paces." Mac slung his duffel bag over one shoulder and pulled out his burner. "This way," he said, leading Connie down a side road.

It was quieter back here. Debris from partygoers littered the gutters and the streetlights cast a surreal amber glow across the cobblestone streets. Connie held on to his hand, her anxiety ramping up. Halfway down, Mac ducked in between two buildings. She stayed close to his side as he punched the keys on the phone.

"What are you doing?" she whispered.

"Checking our coordinates."

Eastwood and Diaz came up behind them. Connie jumped.

"We'll need another car," said Diaz.

"And fast," Eastwood added. "By now, the store clerk has given the police Art's description. They'll be looking for us. We need to get out of here."

Mac shoved the phone back into his pocket. "I'll do it. Stay hidden. Watch over her," he said, releasing Connie's hand.

"What? No!" Alarm filled her brown eyes.

"It's okay. I'll be back...with our ride." Mac patted her arm and took off.

She watched him go, fighting the urge to run after him. Swallowing her fear, she remained in the shadows with her two bodyguards.

Art placed a hand on her shoulder. "Don't worry, Ms. Wheeler. He'll be okay. Mac is highly trained for these situations."

Eastwood caught Art's eye, the corner of his lips twitching.

"But anything could happen," she said, looking out at the now empty street.

"True, and he can handle it. Mac's a Green Beret. You should see him jump out of a perfectly good airplane."

She looked up at Art. "He does that?"

Eastwood chuckled. "Well, we all do, but for some of us," he slapped Art playfully on the back of his head, "it's a new skill."

Connie looked at him. "And you? Is it an old or a new skill?"

He smiled. "Old. I've been jumping out of planes for a while now. It's what Green Berets do."

"Have you ever been hurt jumping?"

"No, ma'am, but I did suffer an injury last year. An RPG explosion," he said. Then, Eastwood lifted his left leg and tapped below the knee. The metallic sound startled Connie.

Her eyes widened. "How did I not know? I'm so sorry, Sergeant. And you're still active duty?"

He cleared his throat. "Our unit is…special."

Connie looked at them both. "Your leg. Art's eye…"

Art lifted his right hand and removed his glove revealing a second injury. "And my ring and pinky finger," he grimaced.

"Oh, Art," she said, reaching for his hand and holding it gently. "You've both suffered so much." She grew silent contemplating what Mac had shared with her about seeing too much, about his post-traumatic stress disorder. "I don't know how you men do what you do and keep going. You're the bravest people I've ever met."

"That's very kind," Art said.

"And true. Sergeant Tyler mentioned a wife. Do you have a sweetheart, Art?"

Eastwood choked on a laugh.

Diaz threw him side eye. "No ma'am."

"Really? That's surprising."

"Well, there's a girl…" Eastwood began, stirring the pot.

"Stuff it, Harry!" Diaz growled.

In answer, Eastwood began to waltz.

"Dammit, Harry, when we get back…"

Connie stifled a laugh at their banter. It was obvious they were not just brothers in arms, but friends. "Who is she?"

Diaz sighed. "Our communications exec. Natalie. Her name is Natalie, but there's nothing going on. We're just, you know, friends."

Biting her lip, Connie smiled. "I see."

"You do?" he asked, skeptical.

"Sure. You like her, respect her?"

"Well, yeah. She's nice."

"Nice, he says," Eastwood snorted. "She's head over heels for our boy here."

"Oh, so she likes…I'm sorry, I never caught your rank, Art," she said.

"It's Corporal, ma'am. I'm a Marine," he added, noting her confusion.

"Corporal Diaz," she mumbled, testing it out. "No, I like Art better."

"Either way is fine, ma'am."

"And stop calling me ma'am. I'm only thirty-two, not someone's grandma."

Art smiled. "Sorry, ma'am."

"Just call me Connie. Now, if she likes you, that's wonderful. And you said you like and respect her. Is she not attractive?"

Eastwood hooted at the look of extreme discomfort on Art's face. He might be able to weasel his way out of discussing Natalie Janeway with him and the others in their unit, but he was ill-prepared for handling the directness of Connie Wheeler.

"She's...attractive," he said, running a hand through his hair.

Connie patted his arm. "Then maybe you should tell her you think so. Ladies like that."

"Maybe I will," he conceded.

"And always be kind to her, Art. Don't ever hurt her," she added, her tone changing.

"I would never—" He began, alarmed at the turn in the conversation.

A car pulled up. It was a dark brown SUV, at least ten years old. Mac leaned out the window. "Get in."

Relief washed over Connie the moment she heard his voice. Without waiting, she whispered, "Shotgun," and dashed out of their hiding spot and into the front passenger seat.

Mac drove them through Puebla. It was the only way out. He'd hoped to stop for a few hours so Connie could rest, but that idea went out the window as soon as the local police showed up. As they came to the corner near the gas station where they abandoned the stolen car, Mac noted three police cars and another driving past them entering the parking lot. Two officers were going through the vehicle and two more stood outside conversing with the convenience store clerk.

Mac turned right heading northeast. Mexico City was nearly three hours away. Police would be looking for them and despite U.S. Special Forces cooperation with the Mexican government, they would not appreciate the mess. Major Maxwell's words echoed inside his head. *Don't fuck this up.* Mac was determined it wouldn't be any more of a problem than it already was. He needed to get them to the embassy, and their officials would take it from there, providing Connie with a visa to fly out of Mexico back to the states.

With the wheels of government being notoriously slow, that could take a few days. But that was still shorter than if they ended up jailed for grand theft auto.

He looked over his shoulder. "Harry, see if you can find rooms for us next to the embassy. Make a reservation."

"We won't be leaving right away?" Connie asked.

He reached out, taking her hand. "They'll need to provide you with a passport so you can travel. That takes time."

"So, I won't be going home right away," she said, gazing out the window, a smile tugging her lips. "Hmmn."

Mac looked at her. Her face was in profile. Most people in her situation would be annoyed at the delay, but she seemed happy. He wondered why.

CHAPTER 11

Shades of gray streaked the skyline as they entered Mexico City. Clouds blocked out the sun's rays casting shadows instead. They were exhausted as Mac followed the GPS directions to the Sheraton Hotel located next to the American Embassy. They passed the Japanese Embassy on the way in and wearily eyed several familiar Americanized restaurants and businesses.

"I'll drop you all off here," said Mac, stopping short of the entry to the hotel.

Confusion showed on Connie's face. "Why?"

Mac reached for her hand giving it a squeeze. Touching her was becoming a habit. "Have to ditch this car. Can't have us caught out for car theft after all the effort to get here. Don't worry. I'll find a place to park it and eventually, it will be returned to its owner. I'll find you afterwards."

Art and Eastwood got out, taking their bags with them. Art opened Connie's door and waited for her to step out onto the curb.

"You shouldn't go off alone. I can walk with you," she offered.

Her concern touched him. He couldn't remember the last time a woman worried about him as much as Connie had this past night. "Appreciate that, but it will be quicker if I go it alone." He leaned across Connie looking out. "Art, make sure she's settled. I'll call you when I'm inside the hotel." He looked at Connie, about to say something, but stopped himself. He dropped a quick kiss on her cheek instead. "I'll see you soon."

Art cleared his throat and offered his hand. "Ma'am, I mean...Connie."

Befuddled, she took Art's hand and stepped out, clutching her bag. By the time she turned around, Mac had already merged back into traffic. But the warmth of his parting kiss lingered causing a riot of butterflies in her stomach.

"He'll be okay, won't he?"

Eastwood offered his arm. "He will. By the time we check in and get up to our rooms, he'll be joining us. No worries."

She shook her head. "I know I probably sound silly to you both. I'm sorry. I just don't want anything to happen to..." she paused, and then, "any one of you. Not after everything you've gone through to rescue me, to save all of us back there in Playa."

Eastwood smiled. "No need to be sorry. We understand, and I'm sure we all appreciate how much you care about our well-being."

"Now you're just messing with me, Sergeant," she said, embarrassed.

He stopped, looking down. "I wouldn't do that. At least, not right now," he said. The devilish glint in his green eyes was gone for the moment. "You've been through a lot, none of it your fault. The fact that you're more concerned about us is...well, it's heartwarming. I'm sure Mac thinks so too. He could use a little care and concern," he said, leading the way once again to the hotel's entry, "from a nice lady."

Art watched her face curious as to what her reaction would be to Harry's words. The blush setting fire to her pale cheeks said it all. He might be oblivious to a budding attraction when it was staring him in the face, but he couldn't fail to see what was clearly happening between his fearless leader and Connie Wheeler. He wondered if Mac knew. Hard to tell with him. Mac wasn't one to give away his thoughts and feelings. He had a stone-cold poker face that scared the bejesus out of those who didn't know him. And even those that did.

Glancing over her head, Art eyed Eastwood and nodded. He approved and by Harry's telling grin, he knew Eastwood thought it was a good idea as well. Hence, Harry's stirring of the proverbial pot.

It took longer than expected to get checked in. Despite making reservations online, the front desk clerk apologized profusely for having only two of the three rooms requested available.

Art turned to Connie. "It's okay. Mac can bunk with us. We have two queen beds."

Eastwood grunted. "He's sleeping with you, Diaz."

Taking the room keys, Eastwood led them to the elevator. They rode up to the fifth floor exiting to the right. Their rooms were side by side. Eastwood opened the door to the first room and stepped out of the way allowing Connie to go inside. It was a standard room with two queen beds. She put her bag down and looked at the men.

"I have room," she said, "a whole bed that will go to waste. There's no reason why Sergeant Maclean can't sleep here. I mean, you need your rest, Art, and two big men in one bed would be crowded."

Art rolled his eyes. "Thank you! I wasn't looking forward to getting to know Mac that well."

A loud snort flew from Eastwood's lips. "Plus, Mac doesn't waltz, at least, I don't think so."

Art punched him in the arm. "Just wait until I find out who told you about that. He's getting an ass-kicking."

Eastwood laughed, remembering Mac spilling those beans, but vowed to keep that piece of information to himself. For now.

Art turned back to Connie. "Order whatever you want from the room service menu. Mac will coordinate with the embassy when he gets back and set up the appointment for you."

Connie smiled, but it was an effort. She was hungry and weary to her soul. "Thank you, Art. Go take care of yourselves, both of you." She closed the door and wandered to the bed, kicking off her shoes, and sitting down. It was dark and quiet in the room, and after so many hours in a moving vehicle, being still felt odd.

She wanted a shower. Forcing herself to stand, she went into the bathroom. Flipping on the light, she found a stark white room with cool tile beneath her feet. There was a large tub with a hand-held shower head. That made keeping her cast dry much harder. Connie sighed. Washing her hair would have to wait. She was too tired to deal with it all. She quickly used the restroom and went back out to the bed. Mac still wasn't back, and she began to worry. On the nightstand between the two beds was a room service menu. She picked it up and thumbed through it. Anything sounded good now, but she didn't want to order until he arrived. She was sure he was every bit as hungry as she was.

Laying back, she stared at the ceiling, waiting. He said he wouldn't be long. Had it been too long already? The bed was soft, and the pillows were just right. Her stomach growled once but she ignored it, her eyelids drooping. She blinked, thinking, *I can close them just for a few minutes. Mac will be here soon...*

⚜

Mac knocked on the door located on the fifth floor and waited. He'd found a place to ditch the brown SUV a mile south of the hotel. It was a crowded market full of cars. He wiped down the inside of the vehicle making sure to leave no trace evidence behind. Locking it up, he walked away. No one noticed him among the throng of people milling about. Wearing a dark blue baseball cap and sunglasses, he looked like any other shopper—if they didn't bother to wonder why he was wearing shades on a cloudy day, that is. He slung the gray duffel bag over his shoulder and moved through the parking lot stopping only once on his way out. Completing a quick transaction, he retraced the route back to the Sheraton.

Once inside the hotel lobby, he called Eastwood for their location. Riding up the elevator, he wondered if Connie was okay, if she was settled. Thoughts of her occupied more of his time than he cared to admit, and that wasn't good. Their time together was nearing its end.

The door opened, and Eastwood grinned. "Aw, Mac, you shouldn't have," he said, reaching out.

Mac's eyes narrowed as he slapped Harry's hand away. "I didn't. They're not for you." He clutched a colorful bouquet of roses, daisies, and Tiger lilies in his fist as he stepped inside.

Art was laying on the first bed with a tray next to him containing what was left of two cheeseburgers, chips, and a sundae. Eastwood moved around Mac and reclaimed his bed grabbing the last of his own burger and popping it into his mouth.

"I guess I have the floor," Mac mumbled.

"Oh, no," Eastwood exclaimed. "No floor for you. There's a perfectly good empty bed next door." He handed Mac the room keycard.

Mac shook his head. "The lady deserves her privacy. I'll take the floor. Just give me a pillow."

Art sat up. "It was her idea, Mac."

"It was?" Mac's eyes were skeptical.

Art nodded. "Yessir. She said there was no reason why, with a perfectly empty bed available, that you should be squeezing in here with us. She's waiting for you."

Mac looked at the keycard. "Oh," he said.

"You need to make the appointment with the embassy anyhow," Eastwood added. "You don't need us for that."

Mac sensed they were up to something. Especially Eastwood. He knew Harry liked to meddle, but it was usually Art he messed with. That was fun. This didn't feel fun. It felt awkward, and he didn't like it. He glared at Eastwood, pointing a finger. "You put her up to this?"

Eastwood noted the ominous mood change. "Me? No. It was her suggestion. Honest."

"If I find out you manipulated her in any way, I'm gonna beat your ass, Harry." Mac took a threatening step forward, his finger now pointing straight at Eastwood's face.

The devilish glint returned. Eastwood held up his hands in surrender. "I promise, Mac. No *dancing* around the subject, she said it." Eastwood smirked.

Mac's eyes narrowed to slits. He knew exactly what Harry was implying and he couldn't say a damn word, not with Art watching their byplay. "Fucker," he mumbled. "Just wait 'til you're alone." Mac turned and left the room. As soon as he entered the hallway, he heard them laughing it up. Silently, he promised retribution against both.

He walked next door and raised his hand to knock, but remembered he had the key. Plus, she might be sleeping, and he didn't want to disturb her. Quietly, he slid the keycard into the slot and when the light blinked green, opened the door.

Silence greeted him. He closed and locked the door and moved into the room. A lovely vision in pink greeted his eyes. Connie was curled on her side, out like a light. He looked at the flowers wrapped in clear cellophane and tied with a bright red bow. Carefully, he laid them down on the dresser and unloaded his duffel bag onto the blue upholstered chair in the corner. There was no food tray inside the room, and none outside the door. He figured she fell asleep waiting for him. He was loath to disturb her. She'd gone through so much over the past few days, but he needed to call the embassy, and they needed to eat. He would begin with the embassy call. If she woke up, he could ask her what she wanted, and if she didn't awaken, he decided he would take his own rest and wait for her.

He pulled out his burner phone and stepped into the bathroom, closing the door. She might still hear him, but the sound of his voice wouldn't be overly loud. He took a few moments for himself, splashing cold water on his face and washing his hands. Refreshed, he dialed the number to their embassy contact.

The Security Agent answered on the third ring. "Garza," he said

"It's Sergeant Maclean," said Mac. "We're in Mexico City."

Raymond Garza paused. "Any problems?"

"Nothing we couldn't handle."

"Where are you staying?"

Mac eyed his reflection in the mirror. His hair had begun to grow out and he needed a shave. "Next door. The Sheraton," he said, rattling off the room number. "When can I bring her in? She can't travel without a passport."

"First thing in the morning," said Garza. "Eight a.m. I'll let the guards know."

"See you then," said Mac, hanging up. They had the day. That was good. Everyone was tired. In the morning, the embassy would deal with the paperwork, and God willing, perform the small miracle of producing a passport in time to book an afternoon or night flight out. Worst case scenario, it would be the next day. The wheels of government turned at a painfully slow pace more often than not.

He slipped the phone back into his pocket and exited the bathroom. He leaned against the wall watching Connie sleep, thinking about the last couple of days together. The simple action filled him with peace. As he reminisced, she opened her eyes, catching him watching her.

"You're back," she said, yawning and stretching.

He gave a brief nod.

"How long?" she asked.

He noted her confusion. He experienced that same phenomenon many times waking up in unfamiliar places after being so physically drained he couldn't stay awake. He glanced at his watch. "Maybe thirty minutes. Not too long. You hungry?"

Connie closed her eyes, nodding. "Yes."

Mac chuckled. "Didn't sound convincing," he said.

She smiled; eyes still closed. "Just tired. I wanted to shower, wash my hair, but couldn't bring myself to make the attempt." She held up her arm, flashing the cast. "It's hard keeping it dry, and that tub has a hand-held shower head.

Turning on his heel, Mac re-entered the bathroom and eyed the tub. It was large. However, there was plenty of room at the far end between it and the wall. He walked over, stuck the plug into the drain and turned on the water. Sticking his hand under the spray, he made sure it wasn't too hot and let it run. Behind him were several bottles provided by the hotel. He picked them up reading the labels. Shampoo. Conditioner. Bubble bath. Body wash. He confessed to himself he didn't know the difference between bubble bath and body wash, but bubble bath sounded like bubbles, so he twisted the lid off and poured it in. Immediately, the tub began to fill with big, fragrant bubbles.

He went into the bedroom approaching the side of the bed. Taking her hand, he said, "Come on."

She rolled over. "Where?"

"To the bathroom. You're going to have your bath."

Connie let him pull her up. "But I just told you—"

He placed a finger over her lips, shushing her. "I know." He looked around the room and his eyes fell on the bouquet of flowers.

Connie followed his line of sight and she gasped. "Are those for me?"

Mac picked them up, his expression uncertain. "Saw them and thought of you. Something nice."

She reached for the bouquet, taking the bunch, and holding it close. She lifted them to her nose and inhaled. She couldn't remember the last time someone gave her flowers. Kevin never had. But he'd given her plenty of colorful bruises. She shook her head to dispel that thought. "How beautiful. Thank you, Mac."

Relieved, Mac smiled. "You're welcome."

Connie glanced up and noticed the transformation. The usually somber, rugged man now took her breath away. Warmth glowed in his hazel eyes and a single dimple on his right cheek winked at her. It was a surprising revelation.

Neither could tear their eyes from the other as electricity hummed between them.

The sound of water running brought Mac back and he cleared his throat. "I thought maybe we could..." He took the bouquet from her hands, untying the red bow and pulling the plastic cellophane free. There was an ice pitcher on the dresser. He placed the flowers in the pitcher, setting them aside. Then, he wrapped the cellophane around her cast and tied it with the red bow.

Connie looked at her plastic-wrapped cast and then at Mac. "Well, that will help some, but,"

He tugged her free hand leading her to the bathroom where he turned off the water.

"Oh, a bubble bath," she said, unsure what to do or say next as she eyed the intimate setting.

He hesitated, running a hand over his head, "I can wash your hair for you. If you'd like. I mean, the bubbles will cover you," he muttered, shifting his weight, and pointing at the popping froth of suds.

Connie looked down at her clothes. Mac noticed and turned to leave.

"I'll wait outside. Shout if you want my help," he said. "Totally up to you. Happy to help. Afterwards, we'll order room service." He left her standing in the middle of the bathroom.

Connie glanced at herself in the mirror and whispered, "Oh, my." She reached back and closed the door. Her mind was racing along with her heart. What did this mean? Was he coming on to her or was he just being Mac, being helpful? If it was the former, did she want this? Her head argued the cons, but her body said, "Yes! Yes, you want this." Still, she hesitated. Finally, she pulled the pink t-shirt over her head and dropped the skirt. Her underthings were next, and she kicked them to the corner before climbing into the tub.

The water was perfect. Not too hot, and the heat seeped into her tired muscles. The bubbles smelled liked gardenias and adequately covered her modesty. Smiling, she reached for the washcloth and bathed. Knowing he was out there doing God knows what while she sat naked in a hot bubble bath inspired all kinds of illicit thoughts. After completing her bath, she stretched out, leaning back. It was surreal, but oddly enough, a turn on. And he'd left it up to her. No manipulation. No threats. No violence. In fact, Mac had been nothing but a gentleman the entire time, seeing to her needs. The only snafu was yesterday when she woke him, but his reaction wasn't on purpose. It was the remnants of his post-traumatic stress, an unconscious, knee-jerk response. Once he woke up fully, he stopped the attack, filled with shame and remorse. It wasn't much different to her own reaction whenever Kevin came near. She flinched. Physically and mentally. Mac might be a highly trained Green Beret, one who could no doubt kill with his bare hands if necessary, but he wouldn't harm her, no matter what decision she made here. She knew it deep down. And that decided it.

She rested her arm on the side of the tub, and taking a deep breath, said, "Um, I'm ready."

Mac knocked once, then entered. The sight of her at her leisure took his breath away.

She looked like a goddess covered in bubbles. Swallowing hard, he moved to the far side of the tub, and taking the hand-held shower hose, turned it on.

"Sit up," he said, going down on one knee next to the tub.

Connie straightened, her shoulders rising above the water.

"Tilt your head back," said Mac, his voice deeper than before.

Connie tilted her head back, closing her eyes, and felt warm water rain down wetting her hair. His fingers sifted through making sure each section was saturated. Then, he set the hand-held in the holder turning it off and reached for the shampoo. The minute she felt his fingers begin to massage her scalp, she melted.

"Oh, that's so nice," she whispered.

In response, he worked her tresses into a lather, his fingers causing sizzling sensations throughout her body.

Connie tingled from the top of her head to the bottom of her spine. Goosebumps puckered on her skin and she had to stifle a groan. He certainly knew how to wash a woman's hair. His hands were magic. Her thoughts devolved imagining those hands working their way to other areas now eager for his touch.

When his thumbs dipped down her neck to her shoulders, she gasped. She could feel his fingertips swirling over her ears and down the sides of her neck, no longer just washing her hair, but teasing her. Part of her desperately wanted him to continue the journey lower, and another part of her wanted to pump the brakes.

Warm water trickled over her head again and he began to rinse the shampoo out. She didn't know if she was relieved or disappointed. But the process started all over again with the conditioner. She was so turned on, Connie's entire body hummed. She wondered if Mac was also but was too cowardly to turn around and find out.

By the time he was finished rinsing out the conditioner, she was trembling, her body aching with need.

"Need any more help?" he said, his lips close to her ear.

'I think I'm good," she squeaked.

Mac stood and grabbed a towel, holding it out wide. He turned his head and closed his eyes.

Connie swallowed and got up. The hand-held was still on. Feeling brave, she picked it up and rinsed off the bubbles. Throughout, he kept his eyes closed. Feeling a bit foolish and not sure what else to do or if she should, she turned off the water and stepped out into the towel.

He wrapped it around her, holding her close. His eyes opened, and he looked down at the wet woman in his arms.

There was an overwhelming amount of male appreciation reflected in his hazel eyes.

Connie felt the heat of that gaze, and for the first time, the hardness of his chest against hers. He made no sudden moves as if he was afraid of scaring her away.

"Better?" he whispered.

The fact that this gentle giant of a man, a man of so few words cared enough to do all of this for her, to see to her comfort time and again, even bringing her flowers, touched something deep in her heart.

"Almost," she said, her voice breathless. Emboldened, she leaned in, rising on tiptoes, and kissed him.

Mac, who'd maintained tight control throughout the incredibly erotic act of washing her hair, felt that control shatter at the merest touch of her soft lips. Gently, he kissed her back, taking his time to explore, to nibble, and taste her lips. His hands began to roam, caressing her back and sliding down to her hips, then dipping lower to cup and squeeze her buttocks through the terry cloth towel.

That action brought more of her body into direct contact with his hardness, and she moaned. Connie was on fire, already primed from the bath, she pressed herself closer, opening up to deepen their kiss.

It was all the invitation Mac needed. He picked her up and carried her into the bedroom. Laying her on the bed, he slowly pulled the towel away revealing her creamy skin and sexy curves. His eyes took in the sight, her body aglow from the heat of the bath, her fragrance tickling his nose, and the desire in her eyes drowning him where he stood.

With deliberation, he removed his clothes as she watched.

Connie's eyes widened, and her lips parted. Leaning back on her elbows, she could only stare in awe. There were scars, two of them puckered at his side, round in shape. Bullet wounds. Her admiration for him grew. Part of her hesitated, clinging to old fears, but a newer, braver part of herself said, '*Let it go.*' The longing in her brown eyes beckoned and the gentle, muscled man climbed onto the bed and tenderly lay his naked body against hers. His kisses were thorough, taking her breath away. His hands roamed discovering every curve and hollow, readying her body until she trembled. His lips explored her luscious breasts, his teeth and tongue teasing the puckered peaks mercilessly. When he claimed her, she felt the earth shake beneath them and could only hold on for dear life riding wave after wave of passion.

She lay in his arms, dazed, awed, and for the first time in her life, she knew what it was to enjoy sex. Really enjoy it without fear or shame.

A crinkling sound burst her bubble and she realized she still had cellophane wrapped around her cast. Mac watched, amused, as she tried to pull the bow loose with her teeth because her arm was wrapped around his neck.

Reaching up, he tugged it loose throwing the bow and cellophane to the floor. Before she could say anything, he kissed her again. A very thorough kiss that left her wanting more.

"You ready for lunch?" he asked.

She grinned. "Are we going to do this again later," she inquired, a shy smile on her lips.

Mac ran a finger from the hollow of her neck down between her breasts and back up again.

Connie shivered.

"As many times as you like," he murmured.

"Then yes, I'm ready for lunch. I'm going to need energy."

CHAPTER 12

Connie held onto Mac's hand as they passed through a lengthy security check at the embassy. The building was nondescript from the outside. Somehow, she expected more. However, the inside was designed to impress. There was an indoor atrium, a courtyard filled with local flora centrally situated and surrounded on the outside by hallways circling this way and that. She didn't get a chance to enjoy the scenery as Mac led them to an elevator and up to the office of Mr. Raymond Garza.

A secretary announced their arrival and took them in.

From behind an oversized, cluttered desk, a man in his mid-fifties, with salt and pepper hair, stood. He was not tall, perhaps five foot, eight inches. His midsection indicated a career spent behind that desk. His features were stern, and his dark eyes missed nothing. He looked Mac over taking his measure, and then just as quickly summed Connie up in one sweeping glance.

"Sergeant Maclean," he said, sticking out his hand.

"Mr. Garza," Mac said, shaking Garza's hand. He brought Connie forward. "This is Connie Wheeler."

Garza turned his attention to her once again. "Welcome. Ms. Wheeler, Sergeant, have a seat." He gestured to the two empty chairs in front of his desk.

Mac wasted no time. "So, how long will this take?"

Garza's eyes narrowed in irritation, but he maintained his composure. "As long as it takes, Sergeant. We'll begin with her passport, take a new photo, but after that, our legal department and a representative from the State Department will want to brief her via Skype."

Mac figured as much. He would be giving his own brief when he returned to command. He reached out and patted her hand. "It's routine. No worries."

"Will we be leaving today?" she asked.

Garza shook his head. "More likely in the morning."

"Oh," she said. Disappointment flashed in her eyes. The morning seemed too soon.

Mac noticed but addressed Garza. "We'll need a car to the airport." They could've called a taxi, but after the last few days, the protection of an embassy limousine was appropriate. Connie deserved no less. The man nodded.

"I do have some news," said Garza. "Oscar Fernandez-Ochoa is in the wind."

This surprised Mac. "How the hell did he get away? Zamora had him boxed in."

"He tried to negotiate a deal with the U.S. It fell through. He ran while several of his own men died."

"Negotiate with what? He had no leverage. We extracted all the hostages." Mac sat forward.

Garza eyed Connie, then hit the button on his phone. A voice answered the com call.

"Yes, Mr. Garza?" It was the secretary who brought them.

"Eva, please take Ms. Wheeler to the passport office, and then escort her to legal. Jones is waiting."

"Yes, sir." She hung up and entered the office. "Ms. Wheeler, come with me please." The younger woman, petite with dark hair and eyes, and a friendly smile waited as Connie got up to follow her out.

She cast a last look at Mac who gave her a reassuring nod.

As soon as they were alone, Garza continued. "Colima did have leverage."

"Which was?" Mac waited, both curious and worried they somehow missed someone. But they had the names. He was sure each hostage was accounted for.

"An undercover operative. The man we had on the inside of Sinaloa," he said. "Your contact."

Mac froze, his expression deliberately neutral. Griz. They got Griz. "You said negotiations fell through." He waited, fearing the worst.

Garza nodded. "When Fernandez-Ochoa didn't get the answer he wanted, something we could not offer, American protection from El tejón, he put Torres in front of a Colima firing squad."

"Shit!" They fucking killed him.

Garza sat back. "He's not dead."

Mac released the breath he didn't realize he was holding. "No?"

"No, but he's in bad shape. He's been taken back stateside. Sinaloa thinks he's dead, and there's nothing we can do about that now."

Mac shook his head. A soldier nearly gave his life and all this desk jockey cared about was losing intelligence. There wasn't a lick of sympathy in Garza's eyes. That told him all he needed to know about the man.

"There's one other wrinkle in this mess," he began.

More bad news, Mac thought. "And what's that?"

Raymond Garza pulled a report out of the folder on his desk. "This man has been raising hell with the State Department since news of the cartel war broke on U.S. news. He's made threats to sue, gone on the local Phoenix news. Says the government is covering up a conspiracy with police to ruin his name and interfere in his life by hiding his wife." He tossed the report to Mac.

Mac picked it up looking at the intelligence printed on the page. An image of a man with dark brown hair and blue eyes stared back at him. It was a mugshot from a recent arrest. The charges listed were domestic assault and battery. There was a cruel twist to the man's lips and belligerence in the set of his jaw. He looked like the very definition of an asshole. Mac read the name listed beneath the picture. Kevin J. Wheeler.

A bad feeling settled in his gut. "Who is he?"

Garza pinned Mac with a pointed look. "He's Connie Wheeler's husband."

❦

Connie was fingerprinted and then told to stand on the red tape in the shape of an X on the gray carpeted floor. The clerk snapped the picture. Connie noted that despite her lack of makeup, it was still better than the first passport photo she'd taken before leaving Arizona. No bruising, and there was the look of a woman who had been well and thoroughly made love to over the past twenty or so hours. The glow in her cheeks and teasing smile on her lips bespoke of secrets, the good kind. She was given a copy of the picture but had nowhere to put it. She didn't have a purse or bag of any type. She was just thankful for the clothes on her back, another outfit purchased by Mac in one of the hotel's boutiques. This time, a pair of jeans, a colorful embroidered camisole, and a pair of casual sneakers in white. She was especially happy with the shoes, even happier to throw away the sandals given her while kidnapped. She didn't want anything from a murderer like Ignacio Zamora.

Next, she was debriefed by embassy officials. The volley of questions lasted for over an hour, mostly the same questions on repeat until they were satisfied with the information she supplied. Throughout the ordeal, Connie wondered what Mac was doing, if he was still talking to Mr. Garza, and what it was they talked about after she left. It was obvious that the Diplomatic Security Agent wanted her out of the office before he revealed his news to Mac. Some top-secret intelligence, she suspected. Information she was not privileged to hear, but her inquiring mind was curious. As interesting as the possibilities might be, what she wanted most was to get back to Mac.

Over the last twenty hours, she discovered that what biologists have long said is true. When a woman gives herself to a man, a bond is formed. It's physical and measurable, and although science explains it as a chemical reaction within the female's body that causes it to crave the man she's mated with, for Connie, that explanation didn't accurately sum up how she now felt about Sergeant Gerry Maclean. She had a hard time thinking of him as Gerry. Mac was already seared into her memory as Mac. But she liked learning his name, and his birthday and age—August third, age thirty-eight. She liked hearing about his hobby of gardening that began as therapy. It made sense that his favorite color is green, and he preferred Asian cuisine over American fare. But that's all she'd learned so far, and that information was hard-won, like pulling teeth. Mac preferred to listen over talking, and he would be a great listener if she would only open up and talk. But Connie wasn't ready yet. And he hadn't asked. So, they'd made love, ate food ordered from room service, and watched movies on television.

Art and Eastwood checked on them once. Mac opened the door when they knocked and was rather curt with his men who, after noticing Mac's bare torso and feet, took turns trying to look over his shoulder inside the room for Connie. She waved at Art, still wearing her plush white hotel robe. One eyebrow raised, Art smiled, giving her a thumbs up, then turned to leave, dragging Eastwood away with him.

Annoyed, Mac closed and locked the door, but his irritated expression softened to a smile when he caught Connie grinning like a loon.

"They think we're..." he began.

"We are," she said, *finishing his sentence.*

He leaned his shoulder against the wall. "Ain't none of their business."

"They mean well."

"Diaz might, but Harry's another story. Always stirring the pot."

"They really care about you, Mac."

This surprised him. "Oh?"

Connie chose her words with caution knowing Mac wasn't the type to appreciate people gossiping about him. Especially not his men. She wanted to make sure he knew that wasn't the case. "Yes. I was really worried when you took off this morning. I know you're a soldier, but that didn't stop me from," she threw up her hands, "just being irrational and scared something could happen. Both Art and Harry assured me you can handle anything thrown at you, that you're highly trained and can always be counted on."

He hadn't expected that. "Oh," he said, the wind knocked out of his sails. "Fuckers," he mumbled, a hint of a smile tugging at the corners of his lips. "Guess they're not that bad then."

"No, they're not. So, go easy on them. They have a great deal of respect for you."

He looked at her then, more relaxed than she'd seen him since they met. "So, now what?"

Connie basked in the warmth of his hazel eyes. Feeling saucy thanks to his steady regard, she stood up and untied the *robe letting it slip from her shoulders and drop to the floor. Raw desire blazed in his eyes as he pushed off from the wall, his hungry gaze taking in the sight of her nude body.*

"Now, you should maybe," she bit her lip, "go hard on me?" she whispered, her words both provocative and breathless as she stood unsure and exposed.

He couldn't help himself and chuckled. "Hard, you say?" Mac approached her, his muscles flexing, his eyes pinning her where she stood.

Connie licked her lips, her mouth suddenly dry. Of their own volition, her eyes skimmed his arms, chest, abs, and then lower finding strong evidence of his desire. Heat rushed throughout her being pooling low. "Yes."

Mac reached out taking her in his arms, stroking up and down. "No. Not hard, Connie. Softly. Slowly. And thoroughly," he said, his voice deep. He settled her on the edge of the bed, then kneeled. "Lay back," he said, his warm hand over her heart pressing her down.

She did as bid, feeling oddly vulnerable. That feeling of awkwardness increased when Mac ran his hands over her thighs and spread them wide. Her heart raced but her blood slowed. Every sense was heightened as he positioned himself between her knees.

"I'm going to taste you now," he said, his tone deep and filled with reverence, and before she could reply, he went to work.

This was all new! Kevin had never pleasured her this way, although he had often demanded oral sex from her throughout their marriage. She was both embarrassed and on fire. All she could do was grip the covers and squirm as the sensations coiled within her belly, tightening painfully in the most pleasant way until she exploded, her body spasming as the orgasm washed over her.

That was first thing this morning.

Connie felt the heat in her cheeks as the memory replayed in her mind. She would rather be thinking about Mac, would much rather be with him than here. When the embassy lawyer announced she could go, she couldn't leave fast enough, excited to rejoin her lover.

She followed the clerk down the hall, ready to enjoy the rest of her day. She had no idea what would happen after Mexico, if she'd ever see Mac again. The thought brought her pain. But she had now. She had today with this gentle giant of a man who made her feel sexy, made her feel safe. Tomorrow, she would worry about returning to Phoenix. Tomorrow, she would plot a way to get in, get her things from storage, and get back out. She'd figure out then where to go next, but today...today was for her and Mac.

Smiling, Connie entered Mr. Garza's outer office. Mac was waiting. When he stood and looked at her, she was shocked to see a coldness in his eyes. Anger rolled off him in waves as he acknowledged her presence—barely. Her smiled faltered.

"Let's go." He walked out, leaving Connie staring at his back confused and hurt.

CHAPTER 13

"She's married?" Eastwood watched Mac pace back and forth in the small space of the hotel room. He'd been wearing a path in the carpet for two hours.

Art sat on his bed disarming and packing his firearms for safe transport when they finally boarded a plane for the states. He'd been as surprised as Eastwood when Mac knocked on their door, duffel bag in hand. He'd pushed past Harry and announced he would be staying with them until it was time to leave.

"Knew it," Mac mumbled. "Too good to be true," he said, doing an about-face retracing his steps.

"Are you sure? I mean, she hasn't said anything about a husband to us, has she, Art?" Eastwood looked at Diaz.

Art shook his head, then paused. "Well, no, but..."

Mac stopped him cold. "But nothing! Married is married. Cheating is cheating," he said, thinking of Paula and what she'd put him through.

Eastwood rubbed the days-old beard growth on his chin eyeing Art before looking at Mac again. The man was a snorting bull right now and Eastwood's usual jocularity would not help so he remained silent. He admitted he didn't know much about Maclean's past as far as relationships went. But what he was witnessing right now was telling. There was more going on here than meets the eye.

He spoke, instead, to Diaz. "But what?"

Art put the gun case aside. "Back in Puebla when we were in that alley, remember what she said to me? It struck me kinda odd then."

"What?" Eastwood asked.

"When she was grilling me about Natalie she said, '*Don't ever hurt her.*' I know it sounds like nothing more than womanly advice, but it was the way she said it. Like she's been hurt before. Maybe a lot." He glanced at Mac who stopped pacing.

Eastwood picked up the thread. "You think she ran away from him? Kinda weird she's down here alone. And the cast too," he said. "Plus, she hasn't mentioned any husband, not even when we've talked about wives and sweethearts."

The wheels spun inside Mac's head. He wondered that himself but had been too polite to ask. About all of it. And he'd left her in the room next door, stunned by his rejection, with no explanation even as he packed his bag and walked out. He figured at the time it was telling she hadn't asked why, but if Connie was a victim of abuse, why would she ask? It was entirely possible she was terrified of him for the same reason the men he worked with often were when he got into a mood. Every last one said he was one scary motherfucker. *Shit.*

Mac turned abruptly and headed to the door.

"Where are you going?" Eastwood asked.

"To get some answers. And apologize. Fuck!" He threw his hands over his head and pounded his skull.

Mac left his men staring at each other, eyebrows raised.

"He's got it bad," said Art.

Eastwood took a seat on the edge of his bed. "He does. And there's no guarantee it will work out. I mean...with what we do and all. Didn't her passport say she was from Arizona?"

"Yeah. That could be a problem."

"So could a husband, or ex-husband. I mean, we don't know her situation. If he's an abuser like we think..." Eastwood tapped his fingers on his knees.

"If he is, Mac will kill him." Diaz finished the thought.

"And that'll ruin his career for sure. Mac could survive prison life in Fort Leavenworth, but he'd miss weekend barbecues with the guys."

Art nodded. "We can't let that happen to him."

"No, we can't. He needs us, Diaz. Shit, we'll have to intervene." Eastwood sat forward planting his elbows on his knees. "If there's an abusive husband—"

"Or ex-husband stalking her—" said Art.

"Then he's going to need a deterrent, a powerful one." Eastwood punched a fist into his open palm making the point.

"A real beat-down. Because you know idiots like that don't ever stop. That's why so many women end up—"

The door opened wide. Mac stood there, breathing hard, eyes wild. "She's gone!"

⇝⇜

Connie stood in line to board the Southwest Airlines flight to Phoenix. After Mac walked out, she didn't see any reason to stick around. She threw her few belongings into a plastic bag and returned to Mr. Garza's office to check on the progress of her passport. Thankfully, it was ready. All she needed was an airline ticket which, after explaining her desire to leave as soon as possible, was arranged by Garza's secretary. The woman asked about Sergeant Maclean and his men, if they needed their passage arranged as well. Connie had no idea, but she didn't think they would be going to Phoenix in any case. Thinking on her feet, she told a little white lie. The men, she said, would come by later to make their own arrangements back to base—*wherever that was*, she thought. She hadn't bothered to ask where they were stationed throughout her ordeal.

No time for information gathering. She'd been on the run.

She ran from Phoenix. Ran from Playa del Carmen. And now, she was running again, back to square one. She didn't know what was worse, who she was running from or where she was running to. Whatever the case, Connie was grateful for the airline ticket and more so for the two hundred in cash given along with it so she could get a taxi home and whatever else she might need on her journey. An embassy driver took her straight to the airport afterwards. There was no time to lose. Her flight left in an hour.

As soon as they pulled away, the tears began to fall. Blinking hard, she struggled to clearly see the passing scenery as she tried to make sense of it all. What happened? Why had Mac suddenly turned so cold? What did she do?

No answer was forthcoming despite wracking her brain. As far as she knew, everything was fine, better than fine, when they left for the meeting with Mr. Garza. Then she'd been taken off to complete her new passport followed by a briefing from embassy officials. When she came back, everything changed. Just what had they talked about while she was away?

Or, and this was the part that hurt the most, had Mac decided their little honeymoon was over? She hung her head low, miserable. Maybe she was just naïve. What would a man like Mac want with someone like her anyhow? She wasn't anything special. Kevin made sure to pound that fact into her head for ten years. She was plain. A few pounds over the mark. She never did anything right as even her attempt to start her life over proved. She wasn't worthy of love. And despite how kind he had been, Mac probably saw all of that. He was nice out of pity, no doubt. She swallowed the hard lump in her throat remembering the tender moments. At least, she thought he'd intended tenderness at the time. And she'd been moved by every kiss, every touch, just like an untried schoolgirl who didn't know any better. But she did know better. Men take what they want, by persuasion or force. Mac's way was persuasion. Seduction. He'd made her think he cared, more fool she. All the while he was just doing his job. The rest was…a side benefit.

Pain seared her heart as the insecurity buried deep inside began to bubble to the surface again. Several deep breaths held the tears at bay. She didn't have time to cry. She was returning to Phoenix. She needed to get to her storage unit and then, she needed to leave town. She knew Kevin would be waiting. There was no way he would just let her go. It was why she put so many miles between them in the first place. Now, she needed to do that again. But where would she go? If she went to her sister Jo, Kevin would find her, and he might hurt Jo too. She couldn't let that happen. No. She had to pick another destination. Somewhere he would never look.

CHAPTER 14

It was late when she landed in Phoenix and still it was over one hundred degrees outside. Connie loved the Phoenix landscape but hated the heat. Growing up in Utah, she was used to a less hot climate with wonderful winters. She missed the cold. It was yet another thing Kevin took away from her when he convinced her to marry him. Phoenix was his hometown, the place he said he wanted to settle in following college. Once he got her here, he found every excuse to prevent her from visiting family. He drove a wedge between her and her sister for years. And the only friends she had were neighbors who either had no idea of the abuse she suffered at Kevin's hands, or they didn't wish to get involved. They were his friends, really. People who knew him growing up. Their wives were friendly and good for occasional events, but nothing more. Kevin put a stop to any closer relationships.

She wasn't allowed to go out without him. He timed her when she needed to shop for groceries. All her conversations with the neighborhood wives were monitored. He controlled all the money. It took Connie years to save enough to break away. Change filched from the grocery money, earned from clipping coupons. It still wasn't enough, but after her last hospitalization, she called Jo and her sister came running. As it turned out, her parents had put aside some money for her, placed in Jo's care, before they passed. That was another thing Kevin robbed her of... Seeing her parents over those years. The car accident that took them both was sudden and the trauma of not being able to see them, to tell them how much she loved them, haunted her still.

However, there was no time to think about that. She caught a taxi and headed to the storage unit. Thankfully, no key was necessary. The combination was digital, and she carried it in her memory. Her mother's birth date.

The U-Store-It was deserted save for the desk clerk. She showed her passport, the only form of identification she had on her person and then walked around the back of the building to her unit. It was the size of a garage. She typed in the numbers and waited for the green light before lifting the door. The silver KIA Sedona was still inside where she and Jo left it before leaving for Playa del Carmen, a quickie vehicle purchase thanks to the money left her by mom and dad. The backseat and trunk area were packed with her few belongings. Clothing, personal items, some family photo albums, an embroidered silk duvet in plum, a present from her sister, and her pillow.

Bending down, Connie felt around under the front, driver's side wheel hub for the spare key. Thank God she'd thought to place it there in case of an emergency. The other key was lost forever inside her purse at the Blue Parrot Paradiso along with all her other personal information. It took longer than expected to find it. She was sure it was right under the hub, but after feeling around for five minutes, it was further back than she remembered. Shaking her head, she chalked it up to poor memory. So much had happened in such a short period of time. A slew of details, too many loose ends to count, and all before she could make her escape to Mexico. Now that she was back, there were more headaches with which to deal.

First thing in the morning, she needed to go by her bank and cancel her bank card. The account was new, one she set up before leaving town. One Kevin knew nothing about. Now that she was back and once again on the run, Connie knew she would have to close it out. Wherever she landed on the map, she'd begin again, new bank and all. But before that, she needed to run one last errand. She glanced at the cast on her arm. It was time to get this thing removed.

It took two tries to get the car started, a bad sign that the battery had run low while she was gone, but once she got it cranked, it ran fine. The battery would recharge on its own. Backing out, she stopped to close the door on the storage unit. It was paid up for two more months, but circumstances had changed. She let the clerk know on the way out. He asked for an address to send the refund. Connie couldn't think of anyone except Jo. Her sister would get it to her later. Quickly, she rattled off the address, and then struck out to find a hotel room for the night. After completing her errands tomorrow, she would say goodbye to Phoenix, and hello to wherever the wind took her.

With the window down and the music turned up, Connie tried to forget something else she was leaving behind. Mac.

There was no closure there. No explanation as to why he suddenly looked at her like she'd grown a second head. Worse, Connie wasn't sure she wanted to know the answer, not if it was going to hurt. She'd had enough pain and heartache for a lifetime.

She turned right entering a familiar side of town. Staying as far from her old residence as possible, she pulled into the Motel 6 parking lot. The commercial said they always left the light on. She hoped that was true because she really couldn't afford much more than what they charged per night. It wasn't luxurious, but the room she obtained was clean. She had a bed, shower, and toilet. It was all she needed to get through until tomorrow.

She parked in front of her room and carried in the suitcase from the backseat. That one was packed and ready for her journey long before the entire ordeal began. She had several changes of clothes, personal items, and shoes. Hauling her duvet and pillow out as well, she locked up the Sedona and went inside. It didn't take long to unpack, shower, and fall into bed. She was exhausted, too exhausted to think. For that, Connie was thankful as the last few days took their toll pulling her down into a deep, dreamless sleep.

⁙⁙⁙⁙⁙ ⁙⁙⁙⁙⁙

Mac's mood plummeted. He was so out of sorts, Eastwood and Diaz made a point to give him a wide berth. Discovering Connie left without even saying goodbye sent Mac spiraling. And yet, he had to admit it was his own fault. There was nothing he could do. He hurt her in the most unforgiveable way.

He spent the entirety of their flight back to Nevada quietly berating himself. Not even the medication prescribed by Dr. Delaney helped. He couldn't numb this pain. And the crying four-year-old in the seat in front of him got on his last nerve. That's when he stopped the flight attendant and ordered a vodka tonic. He hadn't touched a drink in a long time. He didn't have a drinking problem, could usually handle his liquor, but it wasn't recommended to mix with his medication, and he was always the guy who tried to follow the rules. Problem was, somewhere along the way, his heart overruled his head. When did that happen? Was it in Playa del Carmen? Puebla? Or Mexico City? No, he knew when it happened, he just had not been aware of it at the time. It was the moment he laid eyes on her passport photo. That was the moment he'd been hooked. The haunted brown eyes. The raw vulnerability. He recognized her suffering, something for which his own scarred heart was all too familiar.

He fell before he even jumped from that chopper.

Now, she was gone. He pushed her away because he was too afraid to ask a simple question, too afraid the answer might break his heart.

Mac called himself every kind of a coward before knocking back the drink. He admitted to himself that for the first time in two years, he didn't know how to proceed. All his coping exercises were for his PTSD. He never learned to deal with a broken heart. Not when Paula left him alone struggling to hold onto his sanity so she could be with her lover, and certainly not now as he grappled with being abandoned—again. Both times had a common denominator. Him. He was willing to take all the blame, knew it was his fault, but he had no idea what to do about it.

When the plane landed in Las Vegas, he was raring for a fight.

Recognizing a man in pain, Eastwood and Art remained quiet and let Mac take the lead following a few paces behind. This was the Mac they first met a year ago, the one whose vibe screamed, "*Step off before I kill you!*"

They didn't know how to help, but they both breathed a sigh of relief when they saw the familiar face in the crowd at ARRIVALS of the one person who could. Nastjia raised her hand and waved as soon as she saw them, a smile on her face. That smile disappeared when she saw the foreboding in Mac's eyes. She glanced at Eastwood and Art, questions in her brown eyes. Both gave a quick shake of their heads in the negative.

Fearless as ever, she reached out and took Mac's arm.

"Just breathe, Mac. Whatever it is, I'm here."

He snorted. "Don't want to talk about it," he said, pulling his arm away.

Nastjia let him have his space, but replied, "I don't give a shit. You know bottling up your emotions leads to an episode. So, we're going to talk, Mac, and I'm not takin' no for answer." She pointed her finger at his face, an act that left both Eastwood and Art holding their breath, fearing the worst. Having Maclean lose his shit in the middle of the airport was not something either wanted to see happen.

Mac stopped and turned, glaring at the petite, dark-haired woman.

Art covered his eyes. Eastwood froze.

"You're a pain in my ass, Moreno," Mac spat between gritted teeth, nostrils flared.

She planted her feet, hands on hips, and glared right back. "And you're a stubborn turd, Maclean!" She didn't give an inch.

Seeing her steely determination and abject stubbornness, Mac took it down a notch, but wasn't ready to concede the battle. Frustrated, he shouted, "Don't want to, Nastjia!" He turned and headed for the exit.

She caught up taking his arm once again, patting his hand. This time, he didn't pull away. Regaining her calm, she said, "But you're gonna. Suck it up, buttercup."

Behind them, Eastwood and Art stood, eyes wide in shock after witnessing their petite teammate face down Goliath. Now they knew how she passed the Navy's Hell Week training to become the first female SEAL, even if a boating accident on her first mission cut that career short. She was ten times the warrior of most men, despite having only one foot.

"Did you see that? She has the biggest balls I've ever seen," Eastwood whispered in awe.

"The size of Texas," Art added, his mouthing hanging slack.

Hoisting his duffel bag over his shoulder once again, Eastwood put his feet into motion following Mac and Nasty. "I almost pissed my pants. Don't you dare repeat that to my wife...or anyone!" He threw side-eye at his team-mate.

"Oh, I'm going to tell her. I owe you one, remember? You'll just have to catch me if you can."

"Diaz!" Eastwood punched him in the arm.

"And whoever told you about me and Natalie dancing... Let's just say I'm plotting my revenge. And Harry, I will find out who told you, you gossiping old woman."

Caught between uncertainty over what Art was planning and respect for the forthright way in which he threatened retribution, Eastwood sighed, muttering to himself, "Shit."

With Mac a hair-trigger away from exploding and Art quietly plotting revenge, he knew he was in for trouble no matter which way he turned. The only bright spot on the horizon was getting home and seeing the love of his life. Joely. If anyone could make it all better, she could.

CHAPTER 15

As soon as Connie completed business with the bank, she called Dr. Jenkins office. Hoping for a quick appointment, she was pleased when they offered her a two o'clock cancellation slot to get the cast removed. Sending up a silent prayer, she thanked the powers that be. Someone was definitely looking out for her. Now all she needed to do was figure out where to go next. With a few hours left to kill, she headed to the nearest Best Buy to pick up a Pay-As-You-Go phone. Finding a reasonably priced Android, she had the salesclerk help her set it up in store.

Small tasks followed. She gassed up the car and purchased a small cooler, some ice, bottled water, and snacks for the road. As lunchtime rolled around, she headed to Roadie's Diner. It was her favorite eatery and it would be the last time she would experience the culinary goodness of their chicken and dumplings. As she sat in the back booth staring out the window, she contemplated destinations.

The waitress brought out a steaming bowl of the soup with a handful of packaged Club crackers.

A smiled tugged at Connie's lips, the first in two days. "That smells so good!" She looked from the chicken and dumplings to the waitress, a young woman in her twenties with a few colorful tattoos on her arms and a long, black ponytail.

"Best I've ever tasted," she said.

"You're new." Connie glanced at her name tag. It read, Hi, My Name is Terri.

"Yeah, moved here about two weeks ago from Vegas. My boyfriend's job transferred him to Phoenix."

"Las Vegas? What's it like there? I mean, besides the casinos and stuff."

Terri made a face, smiling. "You know, it's actually nice when you get off the strip. The people are cool. There are neat places to visit. The weather is mostly dry, so the heat isn't as awful as what I'm feeling here. Winters are nice. And you're a hop, skip, and a jump away from California anytime you want to visit."

Connie thought about that. Vegas was only five hours' drive northwest. It was also close enough to drive to her sister's place in Cedar City, Utah. Only two and a half hours northeast. And she could surely find a job working in a casino as a hostess or waitress.

"Do you need anything else," Terri asked.

Connie shook her head. "No, I have everything I need," she said, sipping her tea before diving into the delicious bowl of chicken and dumplings. "Thank you. And good luck to you and your boyfriend."

Terri went on to the next table, her notepad in hand. Connie enjoyed her meal feeling better with each mouthful. When she finished eating, she pulled out her phone and looked up apartments in Las Vegas, Nevada. Finding three she could afford for at least the next three months, she made appointments to view the properties. Then she located a reasonably priced hotel as close to the area of town she'd be checking out and made a reservation for tonight. As soon as the cast was removed, she was hitting the road. Plans made, she paid the check leaving a ten-dollar tip for Terri and headed to Dr. Jenkins' office.

Traffic was beginning to back up. Connie pulled into the physician's office parking lot with only five minutes to spare. She found a parking space and jumped out, walking toward the entryway.

"Connie."

Connie stumbled, turning quickly, alarm bells going off. She knew that voice. Fear snaked up her spine as her mouth opened in shock.

He stood leaning on the side of his red Mustang. It was parked illegally in a handicapped space. Straightening up, he walked toward her. His dark hair was cut shorter than she remembered, but the expression in his blue eyes was the same. Angry. Possessive. Predatory. Kevin was not a tall man, but not short either. He stood five feet, eleven inches, but the muscle mass in his arms and shoulders made him seem larger. And she knew the strength in those arms having been on the receiving end of one too many punches.

"You couldn't bother to tell me you're back? I have to find out from some damned secretary calling asking you to come to an appointment an hour later than scheduled?" he said, stalking closer. His voice was deceptively low, but she heard the fury simmering in every word.

Damn! I didn't give them my new number, she thought. Backing up, she calculated the distance to her car. Could she make it?

"We're over, Kevin. That's what divorce means. That I don't have to tell you where I am." She took two more steps in the direction of her KIA.

He stopped, tapping his keys on the palm of his hand. "There's no divorce. I'm not signing those goddamned papers. You don't get to tell me we're over. Only I say when we're over, and we ain't done. You're mine. You belong to me. And you've caused me enough problems. Get over here! You're coming home."

His words chilled her to the bone. He did not even try to wheedle and whine and cajole her into coming back. He skipped that part. Her internal red alert went to DEFCON 1.

A couple exited the doctor's office, laughing as they walked their way. Kevin glanced at them, irritation in his eyes.

This was her only chance. Turning, she ran to the car, her hand shaking as she slid the key into the lock. Behind her, Kevin cursed coming after her. The couple stopped, taking in the situation. They shouted, "Leave her alone! We're calling the police!"

Connie hit the lock and cranked the ignition. Throwing the Sedona into reverse, she nearly ran Kevin over. He pounded on the car as she shifted into DRIVE.

"You bitch! I'm going to kill you!"

Connie turned the wheel and sped out of the parking lot. Behind her, Kevin ran to his car.

Terror gripped her as she weaved through traffic trying to put as much distance between them as possible. She took two rights, and then a left in an effort to lose him. Tears blurred her vision as adrenaline flooded her body.

She banged the cast on the steering wheel. "Goddammit!" Then she screamed. Loud and long. Frustration, anger, fear, and exhaustion hit. She would never be free of him. He said so. He would not sign the divorce papers, and she couldn't make him. All she could do was run.

Pulling herself together, she got her bearings and headed for US93. She needed to get as far away from Kevin Wheeler as possible. It was her only hope.

It was after seven when she pulled into the parking lot of the Santa Fe Station Hotel and Casino in northern Las Vegas. The price was right for the night, and for the next week or two if necessary. Like its name, the hotel had a Santa Fe, New Mexico vibe. Connie checked in and then drove around the lot closer to her room. She hauled her suitcase out along with her comforter and pillow and, dragging her feet, found her room on the second floor. She was exhausted, physically, mentally, and emotionally. She had never felt so alone.

Dropping her luggage, she tossed her duvet and pillow on the bed and walked into the bathroom. It was stark white and clean. Over five hours on the road took its toll. She unbuttoned and unzipped her jeans and sat down on the cool toilet seat. Relief was instant, but the tears that flowed did not relieve her burden. How the hell could she have forgotten to give Dr. Jenkins' office her new cell number? Shaking her head, she knew the answer was simple. She expected to get in and get out quickly. Looking down at the cast, she cursed. She should've let Mac cut it off when he offered. It might not be a bad idea to do it herself, if only she had a sharp enough knife.

Connie inspected it, turning her arm over, and then she noticed the writing on the inside wrist area. There was a drawing of a rose beneath the words. A pretty rose, well-rendered. She forgot all about him signing the cast. The writing was small, and she had to lift her arm closer to read the words.

To the most beautiful woman I've ever met. If you ever need me, I'm a phone call away.

His number was scrawled beneath and then there was the rose, a bud unfurling. But this bud would never fully bloom, just like their relationship. Something had gone wrong. She still didn't know what, and she'd been too afraid to ask. Instead, she did what she did best. Ran.

"I'm a coward," she whispered.

Cleaning up, she quickly got herself together and washed the tears from her cheeks. It was too quiet in her room and she desperately wanted coffee. Swallowing her sorrow, Connie took her room key and the small cosmetic bag she was currently using as a wallet and went in search of the dining room. She stepped into the elevator, wiping away a stray tear. Tomorrow was another day, one in which she would hopefully find an affordable apartment. Once that was out of the way, she would begin looking for employment, and then call Jo to let her sister know where she'd landed. It was the best plan she had, and Connie clung to it like a life raft.

She could smell food the minute she hit the lobby. Following her nose, Connie located the Grand Café, open all night it said. It was busy with the dinner crowd, but she was seated at a corner table. Having people around made her feel less alone. She ordered the Deuces Wild Breakfast of two eggs, bacon, hash browns, and toast, and of course, a hot cup of coffee. From her vantage point, she could see guests coming and going through the lobby. Most were heading to the casino or off to explore the Las Vegas strip. She wasn't a gambler. Losing money didn't hold any appeal but working in a casino was an altogether different animal. She was sure she could, at the very least, land a job as a waitress or a hostess. She hadn't worked since community college. When she met Kevin, she was working as a cashier at a local grocery store and taking college courses part time. Naive at twenty-two, she nearly finished her associate's degree. However, after dating for three months, he'd asked her to move in with him. Kevin was charming, handsome, and she fell head over heels in love. Or so she thought. What she'd fallen for was a man who slowly began taking control over her life.

Her order arrived and the waiter poured the coffee. When she walked in, she was ravenous, but now she was picking at her food. Thoughts of how he convinced her to marry him one afternoon flooded her memory. It was a quickie Justice of the Peace ceremony. No family. No friends. At the time, he made it sound romantic. Just the two of us, he'd said. Shortly after, she was stealthily cut off from her friends. Then he began bombarding her with phone calls at work that effectively got her fired. Don't worry, he whispered each night, I'll support us. You don't need to work. Just stay here and be my wife. I need you. This was followed by sex that grew rougher and more bizarre as time went by. Nine months into their new marriage, the beatings began, and they had not stopped until the last one. The one resulting in the cast. Ten years of abuse, spousal rape, and terror. Even now, her body quaked in fear. She might have left him behind, but in between all her thoughts of starting a new life, he was there, lurking in the shadows of her mind like a nightmare from which she could not wake.

Chewing on her bacon and sipping the hot coffee helped. At least, she told herself it did. Now that she took care of her stomach, she realized she just needed sleep. Connie raised her hand to catch the waiter's eye. Giving the universal signal requesting the check, she waited, watching the passersby.

One moved with purpose toward the elevators. She tensed and her lungs froze, unable to take a breath. It was Kevin. But how? Freaked out she glanced around the dining room. She didn't know whether to scream for help or run like hell. Shaking, she picked up her bag and ducking low, looked around the Grand Café for another way out. She located a second door leading to the parking lot. If she kept to the wall, she could get out unseen. She crossed paths with the waiter.

"Miss, your check," he said, trying to catch up with her. "Miss?" he called again, his voice rising

Connie glanced over her shoulder. At the far end, Kevin stood looking around the dining room. Terror seized her heart when their eyes locked. She looked wildly at the waiter and mouthed, "I'm sorry," and took off running.

She had a decent head start, but Kevin was fast. Connie sprinted down the sidewalk and hooked a left finding her car out back near her room. Shaky hands pulled the keys from her bag. She managed to get the door unlocked and jumped in, cranking the engine. Behind her, Kevin shouted her name. The sound left her petrified, but she fought through it. She backed out and tore through the lot back out onto North Rancho Drive heading south.

Her vision was obscured by the torrent of angry, frightened tears. Blinking to clear them away, she sucked in air.

"Why!" she screamed. Connie had no idea where to go. She didn't have anyone. No one was coming to help her this time. She pulled over into a mall parking lot and slid into a spot between two cars. Leaning onto the steering wheel, she wailed. "He's going to kill me," she moaned over and over again, her head resting on her cast.

Through the watery haze, she glimpsed the unfurling rose. *I'm only a phone call away.*

She just needed help. Would he?

Connie knew in that moment what to do. Pulling out her cell phone, she dialed the number carefully written in neat handwriting on her cast. He might not answer. Might hang up on her. And what would it matter anyhow? She was in Las Vegas, and he was...she had no idea. But if she was going to be killed, she didn't want to die without hearing his voice one last time. She didn't want to leave this world with regrets.

It rang three times before a gruff voice answered, "Maclean."

"Mac?" she sniffed, swallowing past the lump in her throat, "Help."

CHAPTER 16

Mac sat quietly enjoying the view from Eastwood and Joely's terrace. It was Friday night and the couple had invited him and the other members of their unit over for barbecue and beer. Harry and Jackson did the grilling. Harry's wife, Joely, made the side dishes with help from Nastjia and Major Sydelle Maxwell. Mac brought a vegetable tray filled with cherry tomatoes, cucumbers, bell peppers, and carrots from his personal garden. Making the tray helped him organize his thoughts, thoughts that had been jumbled since he returned from Mexico.

The ride from the airport had been about as unpleasant as a colonoscopy with Nasty peppering him with questions forcing him to talk through the emotions running hot beneath the surface. She knew his history, knew that if he didn't work through all the conflicting issues then it would trigger a traumatic episode. That would be bad. It took him weeks sometimes to pull himself back into a good headspace when that happened. Even though he hated opening up, hated more being vulnerable, he appreciated what she had done. By making him tell her what happened, it was like opening a pressure valve to release steam. He cooled down and was able to think more clearly.

But he didn't like that Eastwood and Diaz were in the car listening. Didn't like revealing so much of his past, about Paula, and now about Connie to his men. It's not that he didn't trust them. He did, with his life, but he'd always been intensely private. He didn't believe in meddling in other people's lives. He didn't go in for gossip, and he often failed to ask questions normal people ask each other. It made his circle of friends small, and he was fine with that. To his surprise, Harry reached over the seat and squeezed his shoulder. Art, always thoughtful, remained quiet. They didn't mock him or make light of the situation. Their support was more than appreciated.

And now he sat watching the stars in the Nevada sky from Joely's villa terrace in North Las Vegas. They were far from the bright neon lights of the strip. Out here, it was just the beautiful desert, a light breeze, and peace. After the others went home, Harry and Joely invited him to stay the night. The drive back up to Camp Lazarus in Groom Lake took over two hours. Better to head out in the morning. So, he sipped his beer listening to the light jazz playing in the background and ignored the couple slow dancing behind him. Married now for almost a year, Eastwood and Joely Tyler, nee Winter, still couldn't keep their hands off each other.

He envied them. They really were a perfect fit in an odd way. The Green Beret and the bioengineering prodigy. Harry was a handful, but Joely was feisty and called Harry on his crap. The man was so head over heels in love with her that he didn't mind at all. In fact, he seemed to like it. A lot.

Feeling like a third wheel, Mac got up and headed inside. His cell phone went off, vibrating in his pocket. He pulled it out and looked at the screen. He didn't recognize the number, but very few people had his number. He answered on the third ring.

"Maclean."

"Mac?" a soft voice asked.

He froze. Mac opened his mouth, about to speak, but what she said next struck fear in his heart.

"Help."

"Connie? What's wrong?"

Hearing the urgency in Mac's voice, Eastwood's head whipped around. He and Joely stopped dancing and came to stand beside their friend.

On the other end of the line, she answered. "I didn't know who else to call," she sniffed. "I know you're too far away, but I don't know what to do. I'm so scared."

"Connie, where are you right now?" Fear was a new emotion for Mac. He didn't experience it for himself, but his fear for Connie was real.

She mumbled an apology but grew more coherent. "I ran. I tried to get away from him, but he followed me. I don't know how. I left Phoenix but he found me. He's after me, Mac. What do I do? If I call the police, they won't do anything."

Taking a deep breath, Mac cursed under his breath. "It's okay. Just tell me where you are right now."

"I'm in a parking lot. In Las Vegas," she hiccupped.

"What?" Mac's eyes popped wide. "Where? What parking lot?" He pulled out his car keys and threw a look at Harry.

Connie began to cry. "What does it matter? I'm here and you're...wherever you are. He's going to find me again. I should move now."

"No! Stay put. Connie, I'm in Vegas. Where exactly are you? Give me the address. I'm on my way." Mac headed for the door, Eastwood following on his heels.

Staying behind, Joely called out to her husband, "Call me, Harry. I'll be waiting."

Shock hit Connie all at once. "You're in Vegas?"

On the other end of the line, Mac confirmed. "Yes, now give me your location. I'm coming."

She looked around. "I'm not exactly sure. It's a strip mall on North Rancho Drive. There's a Dollar Tree," she said, looking further around, "and a Big Dog Brewing Company..."

Mac nodded. "I know where you are. Just stay on the line and stay hidden. Don't move unless you have to. I'll be there in about fifteen minutes. Harry's with me. The cavalry is coming."

"Okay," she said, relief flooding her body and warring with the adrenaline already coursing through her veins. She felt anxious and sick, and hopeful. "Mac, I'm sorry."

Pulling out of the villa driveway, he made a face, confused by her apology. "For what?"

She paused, trying to find the words. "For whatever it is I did to make you stop liking me. I'm so sorry."

At that moment, Mac was not happy at all that Eastwood was strapped into the passenger seat of his Ford Expedition. But there was nothing he could do about that.

"You didn't do anything wrong. It was me. I was the ass. We'll talk about that later. Right now, I just want you to focus on my voice. Tell me what you see. Anything strange?"

She was slumped low in the seat looking out. Glancing left and right, and then checking the rearview mirror, she shook her head. "No. Nothing right now, but Kevin was at my hotel." Then she realized he had no idea who Kevin was and began to explain. "Mac, he's my husband. I'm sorry I didn't say anything. I filed for divorce. That's why I was in Mexico. Kevin, he's..." She couldn't get the words out.

"I know, baby." Mac said, his voice low.

"You know? How?"

"Garza. He told me about Kevin Wheeler while you were getting your new passport. Apparently, he'd been calling the embassy looking for you and making a nuisance of himself."

Connie sucked in a breath and shut her eyes tight. Now it all made sense. Finding out from someone else that she was married while the two of them had been carrying on like teenagers must have felt like a complete betrayal to a man like Mac. But he still didn't know the whole story.

"He's the one who broke your arm, isn't he?" Mac asked, his tone both understanding and angry. She felt sure in that moment that the latter was directed at Kevin.

"Yes."

Remorse filled Mac all over again. He had, indeed, been a big ass. He asked the next question even though in his heart, he already knew the answer. "And that's not the first time?"

"No," she whispered. "We were married for ten years."

"I take it he's contesting the divorce?"

"He ambushed me at the doctor's office. Said he won't sign the papers. I ran, Mac. I didn't know what else to do. He said he isn't done with me." Her voice grew weaker. "He's going to kill me."

Swallowing hard, Mac pressed his foot down on the gas pedal. "I'm almost there, baby. And if he harms a hair on your head, I'm going to break every bone in his fucking body with my bare hands!"

Connie sniffed and wiped at the tears. Hearing the vehemence in Mac's voice, the promise to protect her made her feel a bit better. But she knew Kevin. She knew how vicious and vengeful he could be. She didn't want Mac to get hurt because of her. Sitting up, she began to tell him as much when she glanced in the rearview mirror. Parked behind her KIA was Kevin's car. He was already heading for her door.

"Mac! He's here!" she screamed.

CHAPTER 17

Mac gripped the steering wheel with both hands, his knuckles white, and screamed at the cell phone in its dashboard holder. "Connie! Connie!"

Eastwood squeezed his shoulder. "We're almost there. Just up ahead and turn right."

Gas pedal pressed to the floor, Mac maneuvered around a white Toyota Camry and broke a hard-right into the parking lot, slamming the brake before accelerating again. He eyed the rows of cars looking for her.

Eastwood rolled down the window, listening. "There!" he pointed.

It was then, Mac heard the screams. Two rows over near the Dollar General, a broad-shouldered man dragged a woman by her hair, kicking and screaming, toward a red Mustang. He shoved her into the passenger seat, punching her in the face when she wouldn't comply. Mac watched it happen through a haze of red-hot anger.

Noticing the Ford Expedition coming up on him, the man slammed the door shut and hopped over the hood diving into the driver's seat. He took off just as it skidded hard into their row.

Without hesitation, Mac accelerated chasing the red Mustang as it shot forward racing for the exit onto North Rancho Drive. It nearly hit an oncoming truck. The truck jerked hard left going off the road onto a sidewalk. Mac swerved around it and stayed on the Mustang's tail.

"There's a three-way up ahead, Mac. He'll have to turn one way or the other."

"But which way?"

Eastwood sat forward, barely restrained by the seatbelt. "Most likely left. He'll head for the highway. Right only leads to a residential area."

Nodding, Mac hit the gas and pulled up fast on the Mustang's left just as it tried to turn in that direction. The red car felt the impact of the grill mounted on the front of the Expedition. It spun out into the ditch on the other side of the three-way split in the road coming to an abrupt stop. Mac slammed the brakes and shifted he gear to PARK. He jumped out and ran to the passenger side.

"Connie!" he yelled, trying to yank open the door. The door was locked, refusing to budge. Inside, the driver glared at Mac before grabbing a gun from under the seat. Furious, Kevin threw open his door, jumping out. Connie curled in on herself, her expression muddled, confused, and terrified.

"Harry, get Connie out!" Mac shouted at his friend before jumping up onto the hood and leaping straight at the muscular man.

Caught by surprise, Kevin didn't have time to take aim. The shot went wide as Mac tackled the man taking him to the ground. He wrapped his arms around Kevin's neck and squeezed. The broad man bucked like a bronco, throwing elbows, and cursing roundly.

"Who the fuck are you? I'll kill you!"

"Your worst nightmare, fucker!" Mac reached up and grabbed the hand still clutching the gun. He yanked his wrist backwards, his fingers digging in until the unnatural position of Kevin's elbow and the pressure point he drilled down on caused him to open that hand and drop the gun.

To Kevin's surprise, the man who chased him down and jumped him suddenly pushed him away. He scrambled to his feet only to turn and find the large man with a shaved head in a posture of attack.

"You like to beat up on women? Afraid to fight a real man?" Mac taunted.

Kevin Wheeler took his measure, feeling cocky. "This is between me and my wife." He eyed the other man who escorted Connie out of the car and gently led her away.

Connie turned, seeing the two men facing off. Fear filled her heart. "Mac, don't. He's dangerous."

Kevin's eyes widened and he returned his focus to the dangerous-looking man. "Mac, is it? You know my wife? How the fuck do you know my wife?" he growled.

A sinister smile tugged at the corner of Mac's lips. "Saved her life in Mexico. Gonna do it again now."

Kevin's eyes narrowed. "Fucking over-hyped soldier boys."

Mac noticed the man talked too much. "Fucking pussy-ass wife-beater," he said, baiting Kevin.

As anticipated, Kevin lunged, a muscular arm swinging. Mac blocked and threw a punch in his ribs, once, twice, three times before switching up and delivering a side-blow to Kevin's jaw. Recovering fast, Kevin swung again, this time catching Mac on the chin.

Mac took a step back, bounced on his toes and spun out landing a solid kick to Kevin's face. Kevin went down as blood spurted from his nose. Not wasting a minute, Mac pounced, his knees pinning the man's massive shoulders down in the dirt. Fists slammed into his face over and over splitting his lip, cracking the cartilage in his nose, and breaking a tooth.

"Mac! You're killing him!" Connie shouted. She grabbed Eastwood's shirt. "Stop him, Sergeant. Stop him before he kills him!"

Eastwood knew he couldn't let Mac keep beating the tar out of the man even if he deserved it. Special Forces were not only trained in the expert use of all weapons, but their bodies themselves were considered weapons. As such, they could only be utilized on the battlefield, not in civilian life.

"Stay here," he said, leaving Connie by the Expedition.

He ran up behind Mac slipping his hands under his arms and pulling him off. "That's enough, buddy. He's down for the count."

Mac kicked hard before he was clear of Kevin's body. The blow landed on Kevin's knee. A loud cracking sound ripped the air. "Not nearly enough, that fucker!" he spat, pulling away from Eastwood.

Connie ran to Mac throwing her arms around him, crying. "Stop. Please, I just want to get out of here," she wailed. "Please, Mac, let's go. Let's just go."

Eastwood looked around the intersection. It was at the end of the road and traffic was light at this hour. They were far enough into the ditch that passersby could not get a clear look at them, which was good. And since there were no traffic lights here, there were no traffic cameras. He looked at the man lying in the ditch. His nose was definitely broken, sitting at an odd angle now, and his face was a bloody and bruised mess, but he was breathing and spitting out the blood. He'd live. Possibly with a permanent limp.

"She's right. We need to go."

The red haze clouding Mac's brain receded with each breath. He could smell the light floral scent of Connie's hair, feel her arms around him. He held her tight, but his eyes stayed on the battered bully lying in the ditch. The memory of him punching Connie before forcing her into the car replayed in his mind. With her tears soaking his t-shirt, he leaned back looking down at her face. Already, her cheekbone was dark purple. He looked into her eyes, blurred by tears. They were filled with anxiety, fear, trauma. He didn't want to add to that.

"What do you want me to do, Connie. I'll do whatever you ask." He tucked a stray strand of hair behind her ear and cradled her face gently in his hands, hands that were, only moments ago, pounding Kevin Wheeler into the dirt. Hands that were covered in that man's blood.

She sniffed. "I just want to go. Can we go, please?"

"Should I take you...," he was about to say home, but he had no idea where she was staying.

"No," she shook her head, her fingers gripping his shirt. "Don't leave me."

Mac kissed her forehead and leaned his cheek atop her head. "Won't do it. I promise. I won't leave you. Never again."

Eastwood nodded. "She's welcome at our place. We'll figure everything else out tomorrow."

Mac stroked Connie's hair. "Okay. Thanks, Harry." He led her back to his SUV. After getting her settled in the passenger seat, and with Harry in the backseat behind her, he said, "Hold on."

He walked back down into the ditch and stood over Kevin. Leaning down, his expression ominous, He whispered, "In case you didn't figure it out, I'm a trained killer. If you ever come near her again, I will tear you apart with my bare hands and scatter your body parts where no one ever finds them again. Understand?"

The man sputtered, fury in his eyes but a hint of fear as well. Fear won, and Kevin stayed put. Something about the man's demeanor warned him he was not making an idle threat.

"Knew it. You're a fucking coward." Mac spit on him and turned to leave, then stopped. "Oh, and when you get your ass back home to Phoenix, sign the goddamned divorce papers or I'll make good on my threat for that alone." He pointed; eyes narrowed. "I know where you live!"

Mac climbed out of the ditch and headed to his vehicle. As soon as he slid behind the wheel and closed the door, he threw his arms around Connie.

"You okay, baby?" He looked at the bruise, anguish in his eyes.

She sniffed, nodding. "Yes. No. I don't know. I just want to go. Just want to go with you."

He pulled her into his arms. "Okay. Okay. No more worries. He's never going to bother you again."

Connie shook with fear. "How do you know?"

Mac caught Eastwood's eye over the top of her head. "Because I do. Because I'll kill him if he ever comes near you again and he knows it. You don't have to worry anymore," he said, kissing the top of her head.

In the backseat, Eastwood smirked as he averted his eyes staring out the back window. He knew what happened, knew what Mac must've told Kevin Wheeler. It was the same thing he would say to any man who threatened Joely.

Keeping one arm around Connie, Mac reversed and pulled onto the road. She snuggled into his side, feeling safe in his arms. With the windows down and the earthy scents of the Nevada desert filling the cab, refreshing their souls, they headed back to Eastwood's home.

"Still got the cast, huh?" Mac asked, glancing down.

Connie inhaled deeply and then chuckled, but it was a sad sound. "Yeah. I'm really sick of it too."

"I got my knife," he said. "We can have it off before we go to bed."

This time, she wasn't afraid. Leaning her head on his shoulder, Connie gave herself over into his care. "Okay. Cut it off. I trust you."

CHAPTER 18

Two weeks passed in a blur of activity. Connie spent one afternoon near the end of the second week shopping for furniture with Joely Winter Tyler, Harry's wife, and her new best friend. They found a couch, two easy chairs, side tables, a kitchen table, appliances, and a bedroom set. She'd never spent so much money in one day in her entire life, but Mac had insisted. He'd added her to his credit card a few days earlier, then had to leave. He couldn't tell her where he was going or when he'd return, but Joely assured her that was normal for the kind of work Mac did. After experiencing some of what he did firsthand, she understood, but she worried.

Their first week together was about getting to know each other all over again and making love. A lot. She reveled in the way he kissed her, the way he touched her, as if she were something to be cherished, as if she'd break. For such a big man, Mac was amazingly gentle. He was also very giving. Never had she so enjoyed being a woman.

For almost all of the ten years she was married to Kevin, sex was a demand. He expected her to perform her wifely duties whenever he pressed the issue, but he was not gentle, or giving. He didn't care about her pleasure, only his own. She did not enjoy the act. Worse were the moments he forced her to pleasure him in other ways. One particularly humiliating night, he had brought home another woman picked up in a bar. Already inebriated, he slapped Connie around, laughing all the while as if it were a joke, before tying her to the bedpost, stripping her naked, and then making her watch as he plowed the bar bimbo right in front of her. Throughout the degradation, he insulted her telling the other woman his wife was a prude. The bimbo was every bit as ugly as her husband asking if she could slap her too. Finding it amusing, Kevin granted the request. The woman, a bottle blonde with store-bought breasts weaved a drunken path to stand before Connie where she laughed in her face and then hauled back her hand, slapping her twice. The sting of the blows, however, was nothing compared to the sick show the two put on afterwards.

It took a great deal of courage, but she shared that story with Mac. He remained quiet, listening. But there was murder in his eyes. When Connie finished, he wiped away her tears, promising no one would ever hurt her again, and held her tight the rest of the night. Sharing her personal horrors made her feel closer to Mac, but she still didn't know much about him. He didn't pressure her. Didn't make demands. He let her decide for herself where she wanted to be.

By the end of the week, they were looking for a house to rent. She couldn't stay in the hotel room forever, and Mac made it clear he didn't need any more time to figure out that he wanted to be with her. If that's what she wanted too, he added. Arrangements were made, and they picked out a few properties to view, but then he was called away. Joely joined her instead, and they found a house best suited to hers and Mac's needs. And, of course, located in close proximity to Eastwood and Joely's villa.

On Thursday, the first month's rent was paid, and Connie took possession of the keys. The furniture was set to be delivered in two days. In the meantime, she went shopping for groceries and filled the pantry. Small touches were added. An herb garden on the patio. A few potted plants inside the kitchen. Two paintings for the walls, gifts from Joely. It was all coming together nicely, and Connie was happy. Especially since Mac had cut off her cast. She looked down at her arm and flexed her hand. The skin was lighter than the other arm, but she figured if she worked outside in the yard a few hours each day, it would match the other in no time.

The doorbell rang, surprising her. She wasn't expecting anyone.

Connie approached the front foyer with caution. She looked out the side window to see who it was.

The doorbell chimed again. "Connie, it's me. Joely," a familiar voice called out.

Relieved, she opened the door. Standing on her porch holding two white bags was Eastwood's better half.

Smiling, Connie raised an eyebrow. "What's all this?" She stepped back letting her in.

Joely Winter Tyler was a stunningly beautiful woman. Blonde hair, all natural. An ample bosom, perfect figure, and legs for days. But as much as she appeared to be a bombshell on the outside, the inside was even more impressive. Joely was not only kind and funny, but smart as a whip. She was an engineering prodigy who had started her own business quite young. Then she invented advanced bio-engineered prosthetics that so impressed the military they secured her under contract to work for them rehabilitating wounded soldiers like her own husband and Art Diaz.

"I've brought dinner, dessert, and wine. We're going to have a girl's night." Joely stepped past Connie heading for the kitchen. She paused in the living room taking note of the painting on the wall. One of the two she gifted the couple. "I can't wait until the furniture arrives and I see the full effect. That really does brighten the room."

Connie grinned. She felt absurdly happy to be having what most ladies would consider mundane conversation. For her, it meant the world. To have a friend. To have a home where she felt safe. To have a man she was excited to see and not living in fear of seemed like someone else's life. But it wasn't. It was hers now.

"The furniture will be here on Saturday."

"Then so will I. Can't leave you to all the unpacking and whatnot by yourself." Joely walked into the kitchen, her high heels tapping on the tile. She put the bags down on the island and began unpacking. "I have Chicken Marsala for two, bread, salads, and Tiramisu," she said, and then pulling out a bottle, "and a lovely Chardonnay. Please tell me you have wine glasses."

Laughing, Connie moved to retrieve the drinkware. "I do as a matter of fact. Picked up some basic dishes and glassware yesterday. Oh, and a toaster oven," she said, pointing at the pastel blue 1950's-style throwback.

"I love it! Now all you need is a cute matching mini fridge for the deck. You can keep beer in it for the boys and wine for us girls."

Nodding, Connie agreed. She grabbed silverware and napkins, and the two of them sat on the barstools at the quartz-top kitchen island. Joely pulled the cork and poured the wine. Connie opened the food containers.

"Any word yet?" she asked.

Joely shook her head. "Not yet."

"Do you even know where they went this time?" Connie took a bite of her Chicken Marsala.

"I never know. I'm not in the 'need to know' category." She reached out taking Connie's hand. "But at least I'm not sulking and worrying alone now. We can keep each other's spirits up until our men come home."

This made Connie smile. "You've been so good to me, Joely. I'm so glad to call you friend."

The blonde woman grinned. "I'm the lucky one. I mean, Natalie is great, but she's young and she's my assistant, so I can't talk to her about some things. Like couple stuff. Maybe someday, if Art ever opens his eyes."

Connie snorted, laughing. "Oh my goodness, he still hasn't made a move yet?"

The two laughed, chatting about Art and Natalie, and then Joely gave Connie the rundown on the rest of the team, confident that Mac and Connie would be official soon enough. After a great dinner, a sweet dessert, and several glasses of wine, the conversation turned personal.

"I may need to pick up something extra saucy tomorrow. You know, before Harry gets home. He just loves it when I greet him at the door in next to nothing." Joely stretched her arms overhead, then flipped her hair. "Truth be told, I might love it more than he does. It's a real rush seeing that look in his eyes. Even after a year of marriage, he still can't get enough of me," she grinned.

Biting her lip, Connie covered her eyes, her cheeks pink

Joely slapped at Connie's shoulder. "I saw that, Connie! You're thinking about Mac. Come on, girlfriend, spill it. What does Mr. Oh, So Quiet and Smoldering like?"

The blush deepened. "I don't really know. I haven't asked. Truth is, I've only just been discovering what *I* like." She was surprised she said that out loud.

Joely's mouth dropped. "Connie, I know I haven't asked. It's none of my business, but Harry did say your ex, or soon to be ex, was quite the bastard."

The thought of Kevin was sobering, and Connie was having too good a time to ruin it with any thought of him. "Soon to be ex. My lawyer called to let me know he signed the papers. In another twenty days, I'm a free woman."

Joely threw her arms around her new friend. "Congratulations! That's wonderful news."

Connie hugged her back. "It really is, isn't it?"

Pulling back, Joely poured another glass of wine for both. "It is. Let's toast your freedom. And then, I want to hear more about what it is you've discovered you like." The sassy grin was back, and the festive mood restored. Raising her glass, Joely saluted her friend. "May you always be happy, loved, and free."

"Here, here!" Connie clinked her glass to her friend's and sipped the light, fruity wine.

"Okay, now spill it."

"Oh," Connie made a face, the heat stinging her cheeks once again. "Well, um,"

Taking the lead, Joely offered a few choices. "Missionary, doggie style, sixty-nine, reverse cowgirl?"

"What?" Connie had no idea what some of those choices were. The confusion on her face showed it.

Joely's eyes widened. "You don't know what I'm talking about, do you?"

"Well, I know what missionary is, and doggie-style too, but the rest. No, not really. Sorry."

"Don't you dare be sorry. There's nothing to be sorry about. But my sweet friend, I feel it's my duty to help educate you. Hell, that's what friends are for." She whipped out her cell phone and typed in a few words. "This night just got a whole lot better. Connie, honey, we're going to watch some porn!"

"What?"

Joely got up, taking Connie by the hand. "Grab the wine," she said, and they headed into the living room and plopped down on some cushions scattered across the rug.

"I tell you what, when Mac comes home, he is going to be in for a fucking fantastic surprise. Oh, and tomorrow, we're going shopping. You're going to need some lingerie and toys."

She set her phone up on a tv tray, hit play, and then began explaining. "You're going to love reverse cowgirl."

CHAPTER 19

Saturday dawned wet and chilly. A line of thunderstorms moved through Las Vegas drenching the desert. With the furniture successfully delivered, Connie and Joely put everything in its place before making up the bed. Standing back, Connie admired the look of her plum duvet on the brand-new bed. A few colorful throw pillows completed the look.

"Do you think Mac will like it," she asked.

Joely threw an arm around Connie's shoulders. "He's going to love it." She looked out the window at the falling rain. "And he's going to plant every flower and tree imaginable in your backyard. Probably a vegetable garden too. I wonder what's going to happen to his garden on base?"

"He has a garden on base?" Connie did not know this about Mac.

"Oh, yes. Gardening is Mac's thing. It helps with his PTSD."

"I had no idea. He hasn't mentioned it."

Joely gave her a squeeze. "He will. It just takes him a long time to open up. There's a lot that even I still don't know about Mac, and I've known him the longest outside of Major Maxwell."

She remembered the rose he drew on her cast and the words that accompanied the drawing. Mac didn't know it, but she'd cut that part away from the cast and kept it tucked away along with her passport. Her cell phone buzzed. Joely's did too. Her face lit up as she checked the messaging. Connie was slower to pick up her phone.

"What is it?"

Joely smiled, and then grabbed Connie's hand. "Our men are coming home."

Joy filled her as Connie looked at her phone. It was an alert with a code. 411. "Is that what this means?"

Laughing, Joely nodded. "I see Mac added you to the list of spouses to notify." She grinned, one eyebrow raised in a teasing manner. "Yes, that means they're here and coming home."

Spouses? This was a shock to Connie. Did Mac think that much of her?

"The clock is ticking now. They'll be debriefed upon arrival and then it's a two-and a half-hour drive from base.

Just enough time to get ourselves ready to greet our men."
Joely looked at Connie's hair. Only the day before, she had
made appointments for the two of them with her stylist.
Connie's sable curls where reshaped and styled, and then
she let the salon's makeup guru get hold of her. The salon
was followed by a trip to the lingerie store where Joely
helped Connie pick out a few items of satin and lace to rob
poor Mac of the few words he ever spoke. But the fun didn't
end there. The last stop was an adult store where Joely
introduced Connie to the wonderful world of all things
that vibrate. Her embarrassment was only exceeded by her
curiosity. Items were purchased—in cash. Connie didn't
want to put that onto Mac's card. Not one to be left out,
Joely picked up a couple fun toys for her and Harry to enjoy
as well.

She winked at her friend. "Mac sure is in for a helluva
greeting. Any last questions?" she asked.

Connie screwed up her face, feeling both anxious and
excited. Mac was coming home. "Are you sure he'll like that
stuff?" she asked, referring to the sexy lingerie.

"Like it? Oh, my God, Connie, he's going to flip his shit
in the best possible way. Trust me."

Excitement won. "Okay, okay," she said, jumping up and
down. "Should I get ready first or get dinner ready first or
what?"

Joely laughed. "Connie, you are dinner. Don't waste a single minute on food prep. Order a pizza…after." She hugged the woman. "I'm off to get ready myself. I've missed my hunk of burning love so much!" Letting her go, she headed to the living room picking up her purse along the way. Joely paused by the front door. "Remember, be fearless! You're a beautiful woman and he's a hot man who just wants to eat you up! And I hope he does," she added, throwing Connie a mischievous grin before ducking out the door.

Throwing the lock, Connie leaned on the door. Her heart pounded inside her chest. She was nervous and excited. Looking around the newly furnished living room, she knew Mac would appreciate how it all turned out. Shades of blue, green, beige, and cream made the room warm and inviting. The couch and two recliners were positioned on a large area rug around a dark, rectangular coffee table. The windows allowed for an abundance of natural light, but today's weather was gloomy casting shadows. But it was romantic. Biting her lip and smiling, she made her way to the shower. Time to be bold. She already decided on the pink peony-colored satin slip with spaghetti straps. It ended mid-thigh and the décolleté was edged in cream lace. It was so thin and silky it felt like she was wearing nothing at all. In fact, Joely suggested she wear nothing at all beneath it.

"You won't be wearing it long anyhow," she said, holding it up to her friend inside the store.

Connie showered, washing away the sweat of the day accumulated from getting the house in order. She shampooed, conditioned, lotioned, blow-dried, straight-ironed, brushed teeth, and perfumed all the hot spots on her body. She still didn't like wearing a lot of makeup and opted for mascara, a little eyeliner, and pink lip gloss. Slipping into the silky nightie, she checked herself in the mirror. She hardly recognized the woman staring back. Gone was the uncertainty, the fear, the desolation. In their place was hope, trust, and a bit of anxiety, but the good kind. She winked at her reflection and then walked into the bedroom making a bee line for the nightstand. Opening the top drawer, she pulled out two items and laid them on the pillow. She rearranged them three times before giving up. Did it really matter? She wondered what Mac would think of this new woman she was becoming.

She checked the clock. She spent two hours getting ready, but Mac wouldn't be home for at least another hour or so. Connie glanced at the items on the bed. Soon, she would be properly introduced to those as well. Blushing, she went to the living room and clicked on the television. Nothing left to do now but wait.

The wind whipped up again as Mac entered the Las Vegas city limits. A few raindrops hit the windshield but not enough yet to turn on the wipers. If he was lucky, he'd make it home in time before the skies opened releasing the next torrent of rain. He was eager to see the new place. Thanks to Harry, he got the address from Joely intent on surprising Connie. She found the rental after he'd been called away. The mission sent him and the team back to Texas. This time to El Paso. Coordinating with the DEA and ATF, they slipped into Mexico to retrieve none other than Oscar Fernandez-Ochoa. Desperate to live and running out of places to hide from Sinaloa's vengeance, he agreed to a lesser deal with the State Department, the details of which were not shared with PATCH-COM. Theirs was a mission of retrieval. Get in, get the informant, and get him back out safely.

Knowing what that piece of garbage put Connie through made for an interesting dynamic. Mac did not make anything easy on the former Colima cartel thug putting the whiny bastard through his paces as they hustled him out of the Yucatan back north. There may have a been a few deliberate humiliations. A tripping here. A shove into monkey shit there. A few good slaps when the man broke down and cried in exhaustion after being forced to march ten miles in the searing heat and humidity without a break. Fernandez-Ochoa was not used to grueling physical conditions.

He pampered himself with expensive suits, gourmet foods, wine, and women. He was a greedy, egotistical jackass who had reached too high attempting to assassinate the leader of Sinaloa, El tejón. Which proved he was also a stupid man. By the time they emerged from the tunnel inside El Paso, Oscar was begging to be taken into custody. Mac was happy to be rid of him. All he wanted was to get back home to Connie. He couldn't remember the last time he looked forward to something so much.

He wondered if she got the 411 text. It was a simple code command devised for the team. It all began with Joely who asked Major Maxwell if there was some way to keep the spouses informed. The Major said she would think about it. Next meeting, she announced that an alert system would be put into place sending out one single text to let a loved one know the team returned to base. Each member would be allowed one designee. Eastwood, of course, put down his wife. The rest of the men picked a family member. Mac, who had a younger brother still serving in the army, and two elderly parents, replaced his mom with Connie. It wasn't a tough decision. In fact, it was the easiest one he'd ever made. He still called his mom, Patty, to check in. She relayed the news to his father, Paddy. Patrick and Patricia Maclean were always happy to hear from their eldest son. His father didn't say much. Mac took after him. His mother, however, was a chatterbox. His younger brother, Pete, took after her. A real talker, that one. He loved his family. They stood by him through all his trials and tribulations with PTSD. But now he had Connie. Or at least, he hoped so.

Mac's GPS told him to turn right onto Gambler's Lane and the electronic voice announced he'd arrived at his destination when he pulled up in front of number 212. It was a nice house. The stucco exterior had a Spanish tile roof. There was a two-car garage on the front left, and a sidewalk leading from the driveway around to the front door. The yard was artfully decorated with a variety of succulents and drought-resistant plants arranged in garden beds ringed by white rock. He pulled into the driveway. Connie's KIA was not there unless it was parked inside the garage. He sat there a moment. He wasn't a praying man, but deep down he hoped she was there, that she had not decided to leave.

He didn't know why that thought crossed his mind, except...he did. Paula. He did not recognize the signs back then that she was unhappy. Didn't see the writing on the wall because he was mired too deeply into his own pain and trauma. It took everything he had to turn off the ignition and get out of the truck. He wasn't a man afraid to face reality, whatever it happened to be.

He pulled out his duffel bag, slinging it over one shoulder and locked up the Expedition. Mac was suddenly filled with a crippling combination of dread and excitement.

"Move your feet, soldier," he ordered, looking down at his boots.

One step was followed by another until he reached the front door. That's when he realized he didn't have a key. Should he knock or just walk in? But the door should not be unlocked, he argued, carrying on a confusing internal conversation. If it were Connie's habit to leave doors unlocked, he'd have to talk to her about that. He reached out for the doorknob, then paused, letting his hand drop back down to his side. He rubbed his face. *Why the fuck can't I just ring the bell already,* he chastised himself.

He reached out again to ring the doorbell when the door suddenly opened.

Mac's jaw dropped.

She stood in the doorway wearing the sheerest slip of pink lingerie he'd ever seen. He had fishing nets more solid than that material. Her hair tumbled over her shoulders, and her lips glistened. He could make out the outline of her nipples and when his eyes dropped lower, the vee of her mons. Looking over his shoulder at the other homes along the street, he stepped inside quickly shutting the door.

"Woman, what are you doing?" Mac rasped. His mouth had gone dry at the sight of her.

Connie backed up a step, her arms once held wide dropped to her sides then came up to cover herself. The daring in her eyes now only reflected uncertainty. She glanced at Mac's face. His expression was one of shock, and by his question, she guessed he wasn't pleased.

"I..." she cleared her throat, now utterly embarrassed. "I don't know. I shouldn't have. I'm sorry," she said, slipping past him.

"What? Wait," he said, grabbing her hand and stopping her retreat. "You did this for me?"

Looking down at his boots, she nodded. "It was just an idea. A dumb one. I feel silly."

His eyebrow quirked. "Why do you feel silly? You look..." he took a deep breath letting his gaze roam her body from head to toe and back again. "Fucking beautiful," he said, his voice hoarse and filled with male appreciation.

Surprised, she looked up at Mac catching him staring hard, heat in his hazel eyes. "But you said...," she began, "when you came in you sounded like you were mad."

"Not mad," he said, shaking his head. "Just didn't want the neighbors getting a free show." He reached out touching the lace edging the neckline of the slip. He smiled. "For me, huh?" He had imagined the worst, but instead was greeted by a goddess happy to see him. Something unlocked inside his heart. He let his fingers wander up her neck and into her hair. The scent of her shampoo tickled his nose along with some other exotic aromas. She was wearing perfume.

The tingles his touch set off throughout her body made her ache. Moments ago, she thought she'd messed things up. Turns out, that wasn't the case at all. They still had a long way to go in getting to know each other, to understanding where she stood with him, and he with her. Maybe it was time for more straight talk and less assumption. She was willing to try.

Connie licked her lips. "So, then, you're okay with being greeted by a half-naked woman?"

Mac watched the tip of her tongue do what he wanted ever so badly to do and barely heard the words she spoke. In answer, he kissed her. It began sweetly enough but quickly blazed out of control. The duffel bag slid off his shoulder landing on the tile floor of the foyer. Mac pressed Connie against the wall and lifted her off her feet settling her legs around his waist. Every part of him wanted her. His lips slid over her jaw to her neck and up to her ear. "Fully naked next time. Where's our bedroom?"

He nipped her earlobe. Grinning and more turned on than she could ever remember being, she said, "This way," pointing, "and to the left."

Mac carried her, clutching her bare naked behind, and kissing her deeply. He gave the room a sweeping look and commented, "Nice." Without ceremony, he dropped her down on the duvet and climbed up. He rained more kisses down on her skin everywhere it was exposed. "This has to go," he said, "but it's very pretty. Just not as gorgeous as you." He lifted the hem of the slip bringing it up and pulling it over her head.

Now fully exposed, he let his eyes feast on her nakedness. "God, I've missed you."

Connie put a hand between them. "Wait."

Mac stopped, confused. He looked at her, unmoving.

She smiled at the frustrated, yet patient look in his eyes. She'd asked him to wait, and he did. No questions. No demands. For that, she was incredibly thankful. His gentleness and respect not only won her over from the beginning, but now, emboldened her.

"I think I deserve a little eye candy too. I mean, I haven't seen you in a whole week. Take off those clothes, soldier." Connie relaxed, her arms at rest over her head.

Mac was sure she had no idea how enticing she looked, at her leisure, her nipples begging for his touch. But she wanted a show and she was exercising control. Understanding that her past had robbed her of her autonomy, he was happy to comply.

"Yes, ma'am," he said, pulling back and standing by the side of the bed. Slowly, he unlaced his boots and kicked them off. Socks were next followed by the olive-green t-shirt and dog tags.

Connie's lips parted on a sigh as she beheld his muscled arms, chest, and abs. He had a light sprinkling of chest hair with a thin line leading down his stomach and dipping below the belt. She felt hot all over just watching him, knowing he would do anything she asked. When he unbuckled and slipped off his pants, she saw the evidence of his desire straining to be released from the last item of clothing.

Mac hooked his thumbs into the waistband of his biker-style boxers taking his time inching them down. When he kicked them free of his ankles, he stood before her, battle hardened and ready to make love to her.

"Now what?" he asked.

She sat up and patted the spot next to her on the bed.

Heeding the unspoken invitation, he climbed up.

"Lay down on your back," she whispered.

Intrigued, Mac repositioned himself laying back. His head dislodged something on the pillow. Two somethings he hadn't noticed. Reaching for them his eyes widened as he held up a pink rubber vibrator and a smaller item in blue. "Something you want to tell me?"

A blush stained her cheeks. "I've been shopping."

A grin tugged at the corners of his lips. "I know what this one is, but what's this?" he asked, holding up the small item. He stuck his fingertip into the opening.

"It's a tongue vibrator," she said, her face turning more red.

"Just what in the world have you been up to?" Mac's brain went into overdrive imagining Connie doing all kinds of things with those two items. He was so worked up it had become painful. "Baby," he whispered, "you're killing me."

Seeing the passion blazing in his eyes, hearing it in his tone, her confidence skyrocketed. "Not yet, but saddle up, cowboy."

Before Mac could decipher her meaning, she straddled him, taking him all the way inside. He felt the air leave his lungs and pleasure overtake him. She began to ride him, something she had not done with him before now. The sight of her taking what she wanted shook him to his core.

"God, Connie, what have you been doing while I was gone?" he asked, panting.

Eyes closed and her head back, she sighed, "Watching porn with Joely."

"You...what?" That did it. The very idea drove him wild. Mac gripped her hips and pumped harder. Connie moaning his name was the most erotic thing he'd ever heard. Feeling devilish, he reached around for the pink vibrator. Flipping the switch on, he touched it to her most sensitive spot.

"Oh, Mac. Oh my God!" Connie shuddered, her body rocking hard back and forth as he sent her over the edge. Seeing her bite her lip as her body strained in ecstasy was more than he could take. His own climax was so strong, he nearly passed out.

She fell atop him, panting and sated.

Holding her close, he stroked her hair. The peace in his heart was so overwhelming, he felt tears sting his eyes. Quickly, he blinked them away.

They lay entwined, catching their breath. For Mac, it was the best homecoming ever. How the hell did he get so lucky, he thought. She'd done nothing but give from the moment he met her. She offered a gentle understanding of his condition even when he'd sprung at her, choking her when she tried to wake him. She forgave him for hurting her, for misunderstanding her own situation. And despite how badly he had bungled it, she called him in her hour of need. And now here they were, naked, basking in the afterglow. He knew what he was feeling, but he was afraid to say it out loud. And she might not be ready. Still, Connie had opened up to him in every possible way. It was time he did the same.

"Connie, honey," he whispered.

"Hmmn," she mumbled, turning her head to face him.

There was a satisfied smile on her lush, lovely lips. Unable to resist, he kissed them, taking his time before pulling back.

"I need to tell you about Paula."

Her smile slipped a notch, but she remained quiet, waiting.

Mac felt her body tense up. He cleared his throat. "She's my ex-wife."

"Oh?" She relaxed again.

"You've told me about Kevin. I need you to know about Paula. It's been several years since we divorced, but..." he paused, choosing his words carefully, "she left me."

"Why?" Connie asked, reaching out to stroke his cheek.

"At first, I thought it was me, my PTSD. And it was. Partly. She couldn't handle it. Didn't want to. I don't blame her for that."

"But?"

"Yeah, but. She left me for her lover."

"She was cheating on you?" Outrage filled her. What he must have gone through all alone with no one to help him through it, and then, on top of it all, the woman was cheating on him. As far as she was concerned, Paula was garbage.

"I didn't know. Didn't see how unhappy she was."

Connie sat up. "Of course you didn't. You were going through your own hell. I don't like her, Mac. She abandoned you when you needed her the most."

Seeing Connie's reaction lifted his spirits like nothing else ever could. He slipped his fingers between hers holding hands.

"I didn't like her much myself then. But it wasn't her fault. It took me a long time to get help. The damage I caused our marriage, it was a lot."

Connie stared into his eyes, furious that he thought it was all his fault for a single minute. But it was the longest speech she had heard him make. Mac wasn't much for words unless they were necessary, unless they were important.

"Maybe, but I don't think so," she said. "If she left just because of you going through what you went through, I might agree, but she had someone else. That's different."

Mac caressed her palms with his thumbs. "It's the past. I just wanted you to know. So you'd have all the facts."

She looked at him then. He wasn't making eye contact. She could practically see the wheels spinning inside his head. He worried she would leave him too.

Stretching out next to him, Connie wrapped her arms around his neck and pulled him in for a kiss. "I'm not going anywhere. You saved me, Gerry Maclean, in more ways than one. And this isn't gratitude either. There is no place I want to be than with you, right now. Tomorrow. Next month. Next year." She paused, and then, "I...I mean, if that's what you want too."

Mac rolled pinning her beneath him, hope shining in his hazel eyes. "I want you. Can't you tell?" he asked, caressing her cheek. "Don't you doubt it. I do want you. Don't want you going anywhere," he said, kissing her softly. "Still can't believe it."

"What?" she said, smiling. "What can't you believe?"

"Can't believe after all you've been through, that you..." He didn't know how to say it.

Connie did. "After all *we've* been through," she said, "it's kind of a miracle we found each other. We're imperfectly perfect."

He leaned his forehead to hers and rubbed noses, content. "We should send the cartel a thank you card."

Grinning, she nodded. "What a story..." she stopped short of saying, *to tell our grandchildren.*

"It's just begun," he murmured.

"What?" she asked.

"Our story." Mac kissed her again taking his time and heating her up slowly. "Wanna go on a date tomorrow night with me?"

Connie squirmed as his hands roamed over her body. "Aren't we past that point?"

"No, ma'am," he said, caressing her thigh. "Will you?"

Giggling, she nodded. "Yes. Yes, Mac, I'd be honored to go on a date with you."

"Good. Meet you here tomorrow at six. Now," he said, moving on. "it's time to try this thing out." He picked up the small vibe, slipped it onto the tip of his tongue, and scooted down her body.

"Mac!" she squealed.

He paused, looking up, deliberately lisping his words. "And then after, we'll order pizza? I'm starving."

Remembering Joely's suggestion earlier, she laughed. Her laugher turned to moans of pleasure as Mac played with his new toy. Connie silently thanked the powers that be for sending Mac to rescue her as she gripped his shoulders, riding wave after wave of orgasmic bliss.

Later that night, after great sex, hot pizza, and cold beer, Mac lay awake staring at the woman sleeping in his arms. He could hardly wait to start their life together. His heart was full, his being lighter than he could remember feeling. Grateful, happy, and beyond satisfied, he thanked his lucky stars for sending him such an amazing, sexy, understanding woman...and for unexpected second chances.

RESCUING EMMA SNEAK PEEK

Have you read Rescuing Emma yet? Check out Book 1 in the Green Beret series now.

Chapter One

Captain Nathan James Oliver gave the signal to halt, then dropped low. The five men at his back reacted fast, falling back against the crumbling stone wall of the tall building on their right. Each one maintained formation, guns aimed forward, all except for Hank 'Hollywood' Jimenez who brought up the rear. His job was to protect their 'six' and he took that job seriously.

"What do you see, Outlaw?" Ghost whispered. He addressed his captain by his code name carefully peering over his leader's shoulder. Ghost resembled his code name. An albino from birth, his blond hair, white skin, and pale eyes made Allen Williamson the target of bullies all his life back

home in Washington state. He'd finally found the brother-
hood every man needed when he joined the army. His sharp
mind and quick thinking led to advancement, and his hard
work led to special forces training. The Green Berets invited
only the best of the best into the fold.

Nate glanced back at his second-in-command. "Movement at ten o'clock, north side of the street, on the balcony."
He turned back, focusing his night-vision goggles on that
spot.

Ghost located the second-floor balcony and saw the barrel of a rifle extending just over the ledge. A potted plant sitting on the rail hid the gunman's face, but the barrel moved
slowly, steadily, right and then left. The guard was sur-
veilling the street below, probably using an infrared scope
on the weapon with which to see into the night.

The street was narrow and cobbled, and stretched per-
pendicular to one of Prague's main roads. It extended into a
poor neighborhood of crowded pre-WWII buildings more
in need of tearing down than repair. Their crumbling ex-
teriors were beyond help and yet people still lived in them
because they had nowhere else to go.

Their Special Operations Group or SOG had been
called in early yesterday morning. An American diplomat's
daughter had been kidnapped from an international school
in London. The diplomat, Ambassador Robert Rand, had
recently set forth new policy from the White House to

tighten sanctions on Qatar for human rights violations. The violations came through a small terrorist group, Black Jihad, led by Mohammed al-Waleed, that kidnapped five French scientists with the CDC visiting the country to study an outbreak of meningitis in the region. Accusing the west of deliberately causing the outbreak in order to commit genocide on their people, negotiations broke down after Black Jihad beheaded the first scientist, a woman named Lorraine Bujois.

The immediate global outrage sparked public outcry for swift retaliation, but the response by the French president, at least publicly, was subdued. The truth was the negotiations were just a stall tactic until French Special Forces, coordinating with American and British Intelligence, could pin down the location of the hostages and run a rescue operation. They had help from an insider, a Qatarian asset released from jail a year ago. His release came with strings. French authorities coerced Jamal Almasi into collaborating. He was nineteen years old and had been forced into joining Black Jihad under threat of death to his family. The French government used that information against Almasi while simultaneously implying it was also a possible way out—if he worked for them. They allowed his younger sister to enter France under a student visa and enrolled her in university. With his little sister under the eyes of French Intelligence and his mother and father still stuck inside an impoverished village far from the more modern city of Doha, he was caught between a literal rock and a hard place, forced to comply, and terrified the Black Jihadis would discover his betrayal. His fear made him cautious, and his caution paid off in information passed on to French Intelligence.

Nate's SOG had been part of that mission slipping into Qatar with the reluctant cooperation of the Qatari government who buckled under threat of severe sanctions to include ending economic aid. The remaining four scientists were found, bound and gagged, inside a sewage tank on the training ground of Black Jihad's compound located thirty-seven kilometers northwest of the coastal city of Doha. They weren't expecting the cavalry, a mistake on their part, and a brief, fatal firefight ensued. In the end, sixteen under-armed over-confident terrorists met their maker, and except for one gunshot wound in the leg of one of their French counterparts, the good guys and the remaining hostages all made it out alive. As close quarter battles went, it was a rousing success.

They'd no sooner spent a week back on base before Black Jihad, learning from their own miscalculations, and angry at the betrayal of Qatar who they suspected aided the western allies against them, struck once again, this time kidnapping a high-profile target, the seven-year-old daughter of an American ambassador. Since Nate's group was familiar with how and where the Black Jihadis operated, they were sent back in, this time following their trail to Prague in the Czech Republic—information provided by the informant, Jamal Almasi. They managed to stay on the heels of the kidnappers, and now they were hunkered down against a wall, in the middle of the night, in an impoverished neighborhood inside Eastern Europe.

"I only see one weapon, but there's sure to be more guards on the first floor," Ghost offered, staring hard at the three-story apartment building.

"They've most certainly fortified themselves this time." Nate glanced back. "Skyscraper, take the rear of the building. Check for ways in."

Marcus Dubose, an engineer from Baton Rouge, Louisiana, kept his 6'6" frame low. His ebony skin blended into the night offering him natural camouflage on top of his long-sleeved black jacket, camo pants, and black knit skull cap.

"Roger that," he answered, moving fast in the shadows and slipping around the back of the crumbling brick wall.

"Eastwood," Nate addressed his weapons specialist, Harold Tyler. They usually called him 'Dirty Harry', but in combat, it was too much of a mouthful, so his code name had been shortened to Eastwood. "Get into position and find out how many are inside and what kind of weapons we're looking at."

Eastwood nodded, immediately pulling out his thermal imaging binoculars, and hanging them around his neck. He moved past Outlaw and Ghost, sinking low and using the cars parked along the street in front of him as cover.

Behind Nate, Hollywood and Doc, aka Jason Gordon, waited.

"If they've harmed that little girl, I'm going to send those bastards straight to hell with my bare hands," Nate muttered.

"And we'll help you," Hollywood added.

Doc grunted. "Let's hope I don't have to turn my back on the Hippocratic oath." He heard Hollywood snort. "Shut up, Hollywood. I know I never actually took the Hippocratic oath. I'm being facetious. Look it up."

Nate swallowed hard, his teeth grinding with tension. Penelope Rand was inside, scared to death, in the hands of vicious murderers. He'd seen this scenario played out too many times, but this was the first time for him that it involved a child. Knowing the worst in men, seeing the cruelty, the brutality, the sheer psychopathy they could inflict on humans had him feeling anxious and he didn't like it. He knew what it was like to lose a child and he'd be damned if he'd let it happen to anyone else if he could help it.

Nate had always been the calm one, the patient one, but he knew every moment that passed was one in which that child would never be able to recover. The sooner they got her out of there, the better. His hand strayed to the black canvas bagged clipped to his belt. Inside was a small fuzzy pink teddy bear. Ambassador Rand insisted that Captain Oliver take it with him to give to Penelope when he found her. Their conversation replayed in his mind.

"It's her favorite bear. His name is Grover. I gave it to her when she was three and she's slept with him every night since. Give it to her so she knows her daddy sent you. Please!" The desperation in the man's eyes and the fear on his wife's face wrenched his heart. Promising to bring her home, Nate took the teddy bear.

"Six, come in." Skyscraper's voice came over their ear-pieces.

"Six here, come back." Nate replied, acknowledging the code. In every operating unit, the commanding officer was referred to over the radio as 'six.'

"There are two back doors. One is locked from the inside. It's located on the far north end. The second is south, near you, and propped open. I found one gunman at that location. He's neutralized."

Hollywood grinned. "My man," he whispered.

Nate nodded to himself. "Good work, Sky. Eastwood, what're the numbers?" He addressed his man now hidden behind a parked car across the street from the apartment building.

"One family in the eastern, first floor flat. A male, a female, and two children in a back room, all prone. Probably sleeping. Two males with rifles walking the hallway of the first floor as well. A third near the back, southwest door is down, unmoving. Thanks, Sky. Second floor, no families, but four guards with what appear to be Kalashnikovs, and one at the balcony. There's a small room in the middle flat, streetside, where one of the four guards is sitting. There's a child on the floor next to him, unmoving. Third floor is vacant except for the rats, and there is one shooter on the roof, southwest corner, appears to be...sleeping? His hands have slipped from the weapon and he's not moving. Deep, even breathing. Amateur," he added.

"Okay," Nate calculated quickly, and gave the orders. "Eastwood, be our eyes."

"Copy that," he said.

Nate addressed Ghost, Doc, and Hollywood. "You three follow me. We'll meet up with Sky at the southern back door. Stay tight." He moved, staying low, and keeping on the blind side of the second-floor sniper.

When they reached their destination, Skyscraper was waiting for them.

"You lead," he told Skyscraper. "We'll take out the two guards on the first floor, and then proceed to the second floor. Eastwood, where are they now?" Nate asked over the com link.

"Tweedle Dee and Tweedle Dum are leaning up against the north hall wall having a smoke. If you come in low, you can take them out before they even see you round the corner."

Nate nodded and reached forward to grip Skyscraper's shoulder once. The man moved forward, quickly stepping over the prone body of the guard he'd taken down earlier. A long gash across his throat showed clearly the man never had a chance to raise the alarm.

Ghost, Doc, and Hollywood followed in the stack. Once inside, the close quarter battle would intensify becoming far more dangerous. Each man needed to stay sharp.

Skyscraper arrived at the corner that turned into the main hallway and stopped. Nate halted behind him. He could smell the burning tobacco mixed with the stale scents of mold and decay. Voices, low and speaking in Arabic reached their ears.

With a nod to his captain, Skyscraper double-checked the silencer on his Glock 9-millimeter. In order to make it through to the second floor undetected, he would need to drop the two hall guards quietly.

Skyscraper eased down and cautiously peeked his head around the corner. The muted lighting from the pre-WWII wall sconces cast shadows down the narrow hall. The building's age was to their advantage. He took aim and fired.

Four short bursts found their targets before the guards could raise their weapons. The first went sliding down the wall mid-drag, his hand-rolled cigarette falling from his lips and landing on the old carpet at his feet. The second guard, who was leaning on the wall, tried to rise to a full stand and aim his weapon when two bullets slammed into his body; one in the forehead, the second in his chest. He dropped to his knees and fell forward onto the burning butt snuffing out the ember.

"Targets neutralized," said Skyscraper. He rose to his feet, waiting for the hand signal on his shoulder.

Nate reached forward, squeezing once. The men at his back did the same. The stack moved into the hall, down past the dead terrorists, to the staircase. "Eastwood, what's the second-floor situation?" Nate released his com switch and waited for feedback in his earpiece.

"Movement. One of the hall guards is moving to the stairwell."

"Shit," Doc whispered.

"He's going up," Eastwood continued.

"Keep me updated," Nate said before touching Sky-scraper's shoulder.

They ascended the old wooden stairs, exercising care and stepping into each other's footsteps to avoid the creaks and groans of the worn treads. The door on the second-floor landing stood ajar, a brick holding it open.

"There's a fire escape to the right and two gunmen to the left; one facing south and the other coming towards your location. The third is still in the flat to your left and the fourth is making his way to the roof. He's going to find Rip Van Terrorist any moment now. You need to hurry," Eastwood urged.

"Copy that." Nate turned to Ghost. "Sky gets the first guard, I'll drop the south-facing target, and you and Doc take the guard inside the flat. Hollywood, you keep an eye on this stairwell. We may need to fight our way out."

"Yes, sir," he replied. Ghost and Doc nodded.

"3...2...1...move!" On Nate's mark, the unit sprang into action, executing the plan.

A tall, bearded terrorist wearing an army-green jacket and a red checkered keffiyeh on his head stopped cold as they emerged from the stairwell. He just managed to get out a short-string of words before Skyscraper put two bullets in his head. The second gunman behind him turned. Nate stepped around Skyscraper firing off three quick shots from his own Glock. The silencer muted the sounds of the bullets but couldn't stop the thunk of a body falling to the floor.

"The inside guard is on his feet, fellas." Eastwood's voice came across the com link. He watched through the thermal imaging binoculars as the hazy red figure lifted a device to his face. "He's alerting the rooftop. Repeat, he's alerting the rooftop."

"They know we're here, boys." Nate holstered the Glock and swung his SOPMOD M4 rifle in hand. "Time to make some noise. Aim high. Don't put the girl in any danger."

"Copy!" Ghost nodded to Doc and then, with one kick, busted in the door to the flat, swinging it wide.

Doc sighted the inside guard and sent him reeling in a short burst of fire. Nate ran in behind them and located the girl. Penelope Rand was curled into a ball on a dirty mattress in the corner of

the room. Tear tracks streaked her cheeks. She wasn't crying now, but her blue eyes were wide with shock. Rage and concern flooded him, and Nate went to her, dropping to his knees and pulling the black bandana down off his face.

"Penelope, I'm Captain Oliver, a friend of your dad's. He sent me to get you." He pulled out the pink fuzzy bear from the bag clipped to his belt showing it to her. "I brought Grover to help."

The girl's eyes locked onto the toy. Shock gave way to tears as she began to cry. "I want my mommy and daddy," she whimpered.

"I'm taking you to them. These are my men. Now, I need you to put your arms around my neck and hold on tight, okay?" Nate opened his arms and the girl ran to him, clinging with all her might.

He locked one arm around her and whispered, "Close your eyes, sweetie, and don't open them until I tell you to, alright? We're getting out of here." He stood and headed back into the hall.

"We've confiscated their phones," Skyscraper said, indicating a clear plastic bag with three cellphones inside. "Got their pictures too so command can identify them. This one's just a kid, for God's sake." He pointed at the dead young man lying on the floor who'd been guarding the little girl. He couldn't have been much more than seventeen.

"Al-Waleed isn't among them," Nate said, looking at the faces of the dead.

"Jihadis coming your way, Six." Eastwood warned.

"Copy that," said Nate. "Do we have time to get back down the stairs?"

"No. Either shoot your way out or take the fire escape," he said.

"Damn." Nate locked eyes with Ghost who, without needing to hear the words, knew Outlaw had already decided the safest route out was down the fire escape. It was for the girl's own safety. Otherwise, they wouldn't hesitate to take on the remaining two terrorists.

"Uh, Six?" Eastwood's voice came over the com link once again. "There's a jeep coming up the road." Everyone froze. Eastwood whispered, "And they're parking in front of the building. There's one, two, three more coming through the front door, and the family on the first floor is starting to move. You got company, son." He picked up his night vision goggles training them on the three exiting the jeep. "Son of a bitch! It's al-Waleed."

Nate cursed under his breath. "Fire escape, now!"

Ghost, Doc, and Skyscraper reached the window first. Skyscraper threw the locks and lifted the pane. He locked it into place. Ghost and Doc slipped through to the rickety metal landing. They released the ladder. The screech of rusted metal as it rolled down unused tracks sounded loud enough to wake the dead.

"You first, Doc. I don't think that platform will hold all of us at once." Nate sent Doc down. Behind them, Hollywood stood next to Outlaw, his M4 trained on the door to the stairwell. He could hear the booted footsteps coming their way.

"Outlaw?"

"Drop anyone who comes through, Hollywood."

Eastwood chimed in over the com. "The family inside just let al-Waleed in. They're in the hall. The man from the downstairs flat is communicating via walkie-talkie to the other two about to land on your floor."

Hollywood tensed. The door swung wide and a hail of bullets flew. Skyscraper countered on Hollywood's left, dropping low and taking the first gunman out at the knees.

The terrorist behind him held back, taking cover behind the doorway.

"Ghost, get down that ladder!" Nate shouted. As soon as Ghost began his descent, Nate slipped through the window, clutching Penelope to him. "Don't be afraid, Penelope. I've got you. Your mom and dad are waiting for you. I promise you're going to see them." His heart pounded, and he prayed he would be able to keep that promise.

Gunfire filled their ears.

"Two men are coming out the front, Six. They're heading your way." Eastwood gave the play by play.

On the ground, Doc and Ghost got into position to defend their location. Nate looked down at his men. It was a twenty-foot drop from the landing. With the child in his arms, his hands weren't free to climb down or shoot. Time for a change of position.

Squatting down, Nate set Penelope on her feet. He gripped her small shoulders and spoke gently. "I need you to climb onto my back, sweetie, and wrap your arms around my neck. Whatever you do, don't let go, okay?" He turned, reaching back and pointing. "Up you go, as fast as you can. And keep your eyes closed!"

The fear on the girl's face did not stop her from listening to Nate. She scrambled up, wrapping herself tight and clinging for dear life. "Good girl, Penelope. We're going down the ladder now. If you feel yourself starting to slip, just say so and I'll stop and pull you back up, okay?"

"Okay," she whispered. Rapid fire gunshots inside the building startled the child who whimpered.

"It's going to be okay." Nate patted her hands which were locked around his neck, practically choking him. He was proud of her fortitude and in awe she'd managed not to scream. She was a brave girl. She reminded him of Jessica...and Charlie—but he couldn't think about that now.

He turned and gripped the railing, descending the narrow, rusted-out ladder. Above him, Skyscraper and Hollywood held one terrorist at bay. Below, Ghost and Doc engaged the two that came into view from the corner of the crumbling brick walls. Nate's heart seized in his chest. He was used to bullets and could deal with it if one struck him, but the idea of Penelope getting caught in the crossfire had him in a near-panic to get to cover quickly.

Doc drew near, putting himself between any incoming bullets and the child on Nate's back as his captain jumped the last foot off the ladder.

Immediately, Nate turned, swinging his M4 in hand. He touched the com button at his shoulder. "Hollywood, send that bastard to hell."

A static voice answered. "With pleasure."

Above, Skyscraper oozed through the window out onto the landing. Hollywood's leg came through and he was halfway out when Skyscraper dropped down the ladder in one smooth move holding the rails while digging the heels of his boots into the lower, outside railing.

Behind him, Hollywood shouted, "Fire in the hole!" and leaping over the rail, jumped twenty feet to the ground, landing in a practiced roll before covering his head. Skyscraper ducked as did Ghost and Doc. Nate had moved as far from the building as possible pulling Penelope around and into his arms as he hit the dirt, covering her with his body. A loud explosion split the night. Debris rained down, bits of wood, brick, and glass—all potential deadly projectiles.

The two terrorists near the front of the building, who'd been shooting at them, were blown back abruptly. With ears ringing, Nate's men got up, preparing to run for it. They had a two-block sprint ahead of them to the truck they'd left parked on a residential street. It was on the corner near the main road that would lead them out of Prague. Unfortunately, the two terrorists had also recovered. Shots fired anew.

Ghost and Skyscraper took point with Ghost shouting over his shoulder. "Outlaw, take her around back to the other side. We got these two!"

Nate nodded, tapping Hollywood and Doc as he passed. "You two with me." They immediately flanked him with Doc in front on point and Hollywood securing their back.

Moving fast, they stepped over and around fallen blocks of brick and metal from the fire escape to the backside of the building where they'd initially entered. Working their way south, they cleared the corner coming around to the street. All around them, windows were lighting up as curious neighbors tried to catch a peek at what was going on.

The gunfight continued. Nate, Doc, and Hollywood reached the street, running across and ducking behind a parked car. Nate lowered Penelope to the concrete, running his hands down her arms and legs, checking for wounds.

"You okay? Any pain anywhere?"

She shook her head. "No. But my ears are ringing."

Nate cupped the sides of her head. "That'll go away. But you can hear me, right?"

"Yes," she nodded.

Relief flooded him. The girl was unharmed and responding well, all considered. "I need you to go with my friend here. His name is Doc. He's a really nice guy. He's going to take you to the truck. I'll be right behind you too so don't worry." He looked over her shoulder at Doc. "Get her to the truck, get it running. I'm gonna help get Skyscraper and Ghost free of that ambush. Hollywood, protect their backs."

"Always, Outlaw," he answered.

Penelope looked at Doc who smiled at her, his dimples deepening, a favorite trait of the ladies in his life. The girl smiled back and tentatively reached up, sticking the tip of her finger into one.

"And another one falls," chuckled Hollywood, shaking his head. "Young, old. Doesn't matter. The girls love the dimples, Doc." He shook his head.

Doc snorted. "Blame my mama. She gave 'em to me. And by the way," he said to Penelope, "my given name is Jason."

"I like Doc," she said.

"Then Doc it is, missy. You ready?" He held out his arms. "We're gonna need to go fast so that means I'll have to carry you."

She stepped into his arms. "Okay, Doc."

"Okay, then. Let's roll." He lifted her and holding her close, took off running. Hollywood followed, protecting their back.

Nate watched them go and then turned, staying low and moving fast up the street. He found Eastwood stationed behind an old green Volkswagon. "It's time we rescue those two before the entire neighborhood and local police are on us. Ready?"

Eastwood grinned, lifting his rifle, cocked and locked. "About time. I was getting a little bored over here just watching like some kind of pervert."

"I thought you liked to watch," Nate chuckled, M4 aimed as they crossed the road coming up behind the two Black Jihad terrorists.

"You ain't pretty enough for my tastes."

"That hurt."

Nate squeezed the trigger and the first man fell forward; surprise forever frozen on his face. The second man turned halfway before Eastwood dropped him.

Ghost and Skyscraper quickly joined them.

"What took you so long?" Ghost asked.

Nate grinned. "You're welcome. Now let's get the hell out of here before we have to explain to the local authorities just what we're doing in Prague."

As they took off, Nate noticed Eastwood looking towards the front of the building. "What is it?"

He shook his head. "Al-Waleed. None of these guys we dropped was him. He's still in there."

Nate tensed. He wanted to get the bastard, but there was no time, and they needed to get Penelope Rand completely out. That was their mission. A snatch and grab rescue operation, not a seek and destroy. Still, it grated. The man had kidnapped a child. He'd also ordered a woman beheaded, a fate he knew might have been Penelope's had they not found her—or worse. He was a monster and monsters needed to be put down. Al-Waleed would elude them again as he'd been doing for the past year, crossing the unchecked borders in eastern and western Europe. Once upon a time, he'd been all for more open borders, but after years of watching terrorists come and go as they please, setting up cells in cities and blowing up innocent civilians with IEDs, he'd long since decided that tight, heavily restricted borders were the answer to help keep the menace of these religious extremists in check.

"Dammit, there's nothing we can do right now, Eastwood." He stared hard at the darkened doorway wishing the man would show himself for one moment. That's all it would take to put a bullet in his skull. A siren in the distance pulled Nate back to the moment.

"We gotta go, Outlaw," Ghost grabbed his arm.

Shrugging off his second-in-command, Nate turned. His men fell in line behind him, and the stack moved with precision in the shadows to the waiting truck.

CHECKPOINT, BERLIN BOOK 1 SNEAK PEEK

Love romance, intrigue, and crime?

Check out this steamy international crime series from Best-selling Author Michele E. Gwynn.

Sneak Peek at Book 1 of 4, Exposed: The Education of Sarah Brown

Prologue

*B*erlin, Germany
Fall, 2013

He was beautiful. Absolutely the embodiment of divine creation with his golden curls, blue eyes, and the promise of perfect cheekbones beneath a touch of what people refer to as lingering baby fat. It wasn't fat, per se, but the roundness of youth on the boy's face that would fade away in another year or so. At fourteen, he was angelic. Striking. One could almost see the bones stretching and growing like a young sapling that would one day be a mighty oak tree. For now, they lacked the musculature of a grown man. The limbs were long and the back straight. His blue eyes sparkled when he laughed and were fringed with thick, dark-blond lashes. His cheeks were painted naturally with two spots of color, and his lips, as they spread across his face with a hearty laugh, were lush and full. Even his teeth were pearly white. Perfection.

The sight of him took the man's breath away.

The boy was tossing a ball to a young woman with red hair. She was older, a sister. Just as lovely and striking, but not so much as the boy. The man watched as the two played a game of catch in the park. He had come to this park every day in the last two weeks since he first sighted the glorious creature. On the third day, they returned with a Frisbee and a picnic lunch. He followed them that day as he did today. They left, and the man trailed them, walking far enough behind not to be noticed, casually swinging his cane as if enjoying an afternoon stroll.

They lived in an old, faded yellow apartment building with too many units to discover which one was theirs. He waited. Two hours later, she left carrying a black duffel bag over her shoulder. He followed her for four blocks where she took the stairs down to the tube and hopped into a car that took them deep into the industrial center of the city. Tourists didn't frequent this side of Berlin. Here, native Berliners came out to party at the clubs and to indulge themselves in the bars. Then there were the others who blended into the hip party crowd, but then slipped down back alley stairwells to a world most didn't know existed. That's where she went now without hesitation.

He waited, then followed. The staircase led to a steel door painted black. The logo at eye level was three large letters—XXX—painted red. Above those in bright neon yellow were the words 'Club Sexo.' He went inside and was greeted by a glass-enclosed ticket booth which contained a shirtless, dark-haired man wearing a leather collar decorated with metal studs sitting behind the counter. To the left was a door, but it was closed.

"You have an appointment?" he asked.

"No. No, I don't." The man stood there, looking at the list of club rules hanging on the wall behind the host inside the ticket booth.

"You have to have an appointment." Shirtless pointed at the rules behind him. Sure enough, that was rule number one.

"How do I make an appointment?" the man asked.

Shirtless gave an assessing glance to the man in the suit. He noted the gentleman dressed well; seemed distinguished, even, with his groomed white goatee and hair accented by dark eyebrows above cold blue eyes. His accent wasn't quite German; more like Dutch. Still, he looked much like the caliber of men who came and went nightly.

"You go online to this website." He handed him a business card through the dip under the glass window. "Pick who you wish to see, whatever your particular thing is. All our dommes have bios that describe their specialties. We take all major credit cards, and you pay up front online before walking through that door. The charge shows up as CX3 LLC to protect your privacy. Once your appointment is made, you'll receive a confirmation email or text, your choice, and you just show up. Oh, and no refunds."

"Thank you." The man took the card and put it in his inside breast pocket. He tipped his hat and left.

He made his way back to the UBahn in the quickly falling temperature and found the tube heading back toward the side of town where he was staying. Once back in his room, he shed his suit jacket and pulled the card out of his pocket. He set down his cap and cane next to the jacket. Sitting on the edge of his bed, he pulled out his mobile and surfed the internet for the website on the card.

The splash page asked him if he was over eighteen and to press 'Continue' to indicate he was, and that he accepted the rules for the site. He chuckled to himself. Beyond the firewall was an 'About Us' section and an icon for 'Our Talent.' He tapped that key. Several images popped up of women in various bondage costumes looking alternately fierce and sexy. He found them amusing. Scrolling through, one image stood out. A red-haired woman in red lace bra and panties wearing thigh high red leather boots. She had a red leather riding crop in her hands and appeared to be smacking it on her palm suggestively. Mistress Elsa, it read.

He tapped her image, and her bio sprang up. *Mistress Elsa is an experienced Domme in the art of bondage for beginners to professional submissives to include extreme roping. Mistress Elsa will bind you, beat you, and/or humiliate you. Your pain is her pleasure. Make your appointment today.*

The man smiled. He changed screens to NOTES and typed. Message saved, he put the card into his wallet and tossed it onto the bedside table. He thought about the boy and young woman. His thoughts went to dark places. Feeling edgy, he stood, picking up his jacket, swinging it over his shoulders, and sliding his arms in.

He grabbed his cap and cane. Walking toward the door, he checked his breast pocket for his room key card. Satisfied it was there, he left.

Out on the street, he turned right and headed toward the tube station. A ten-minute ride south and he was stepping onto the platform. He pulled his coat tighter around him.

The night air was cool in September. Up the stairs and onto the street the wind met him head on. This was not a decent side of town. This was a slightly seedier area of Berlin right on the edge of the best tourist spots. Here, prostitutes plied their trade. Women from Eastern Europe ended up trapped in this lifestyle after being brought in by sex traffickers. Most were strung out on drugs. They looked dirty, ragged, and pathetic, old before their time, and used up. The man walked past these women in their platform heels and short bargain basement skirts as they called out to him.

One block beyond he came upon a few young hustlers. Three of them. One was a tall, lean black boy with a shaved head. His shoulders were broad and his arms muscular. *Not him.* The second one had dark hair and a feminine stance. He smoked a cigarette while talking and gesturing wildly with his hands. *Italian. No good. And too many facial piercings.* The third one was more clean-cut with short blond hair. His jaw was squared, and he had a dimple in his chin. This one hadn't quite yet filled out. His limbs were slim and well-formed, and he wasn't overly tall, either. He appeared to be about seventeen, maybe eighteen. *He would do.*

The man walked over and asked the blond male for a cigarette. The other two hustlers gave him the once-over, noting the quality cut of his clothing, their expressions envious. They waved at their friend and moved off, leaving him alone with the man.

* * *

Berlin, Germany
Nighttime

The temperature dropped as soon as the sun went down. Anthony de Luca walked around downtown, trying to capture the nightlife of the city on camera. The images would be part of an article he'd been contracted to write for an online tour guide about Berlin. He was being paid for the job, compensated for his hotel and expenditures, and they promised to promote his guidebooks. He was famous for unearthing the unusual about any city he photographed along with the normal tourist sites. With that in mind, he found himself on a side of town that wasn't quite the best. Still, it was all part of Berlin.

For fun, he'd photographed a few street walkers trying to lure in some business. They were bold, approaching cars as they slowed down to ogle the local 'talent.'

As he aimed and clicked the shutter, he noticed a distinguished looking man walking quickly out of a back alley with a young blond man following behind him. The blond was walking fast and shouting at the man in the cap. He was speaking in rapid German, so Anthony had no idea what he was saying, but he seemed pissed.

The blond reached out and grabbed the gentleman's arm and tugged. That was when Anthony noticed the cane in the older man's other hand. That cane came around and connected with the blond's head -- hard.

Shocked, Anthony aimed his camera again, and began shooting picture after picture. The older man continued to strike the younger one on the head, back, shoulders, and legs just outside the alley. Bleeding now, the blond raised his arms to fend off the blows while trying to land a couple of weak punches. He wasn't strong enough to defend himself against the older man.

Two men came running, one black and the other white with dark hair, and chased off the older man. Anthony kept shooting.

As he half-walked, half-ran away, the older gentleman looked around him. His eyes landed on Anthony standing across the street with the camera in his hands. The slightly panicked look changed to one of dark anger.

"Shit!" Anthony turned and ran back toward the city center. He didn't wait around to see whether the older man would follow him.

The man tried to follow, but Anthony was soon swallowed up into the crowd, gone.

The old gentleman stopped to catch his breath. He wasn't worried that the blond hustler would report him to the police for not paying for play. He hadn't intended not to pay him but discovered too late that he'd left his wallet in his room on the bedside table. No other way to deal with that situation since the deed was done, but someone else might report him to the police. Someone else with an expensive camera, who was not a prostitute trying to protect himself. Someone who was most likely legitimate. Someone who now had his image on film committing a crime.

He'd have to leave Germany sooner than he planned. He'd have to leave that night; leave before he could set up a meeting with Mistress Elsa. A sigh escaped his thin lips.

As he pondered the situation, a Volkswagon with a familiar blue stripe and the word, *POLIZEI*, across the doors drove by, slowing down. The driver, a cop with hard, dark eyes and graying hair at his temples peered out, watching. Next to him, his partner, a woman, checked the road ahead, scanning the sidewalks. The man offered a brief smile and gave a slight nod of his head before continuing down the street at a leisurely pace. The police car made its way another block down before turning right and disappearing out of sight.

The man exhaled, whipping a handkerchief out of his coat pocket and mopping his forehead. It was a close call, one he intended not to repeat. He hailed a taxi. A quick trip back to his hotel had him packed and off to Tegel within the hour. He had no time to spare. If the man with the camera had reported him to the *Polizei*, his image would be on an all-points bulletin shortly, and he'd be unable to get out of the country and back home. He'd find another way to gain what he wanted.

Chapter One

The flight was long—twelve hours and forty minutes long to be exact—and that didn't include getting to the airport two and half hours early for an international flight. *Thank God for being able to afford first class*, thought Sarah Brown. *Otherwise, I might have never gotten any sleep.* This was her very first transatlantic flight, first any-kind of flight. Despite the stress of the past several weeks, she was enjoying herself, even relaxing finally.

As the Boeing 747 flew her to a new chapter in her life, she reflected back over the last five years. Her mother, Mary, developed breast cancer, a condition she blamed on her husband's animal lust, something she grew to believe, more as the years passed, was a sin against God outside the need for procreation. After Sarah was born, her mother found more reasons and ways to avoid intimacy with Ed Brown, eventually driving him to seeking sex elsewhere. Unfortunately, for Mary, this also led to Ed finding love, and eventually leaving her. Still, Mary would not grant him a divorce. Instead, she maintained all of the financial security of marriage without the benefit of a loving partner. Her fundamentalist mentality grew along with her bitterness, which she heaped upon her only daughter, Sarah.

For her part, the young blonde-haired, brown-eyed girl kept to herself, having few friends due to the embarrassment of having a mother who preached at them about their sinful ways. When others around her began dating, Sarah spent her time in the local library, reading. Anything to avoid being dragged off to the Church of Christ alongside her mother. It was there, she'd discovered romance novels. That was Sarah's only introduction to relationships, and when she'd turned eighteen and could check out books from the adult section, her only education about sex.

After Mary's diagnosis, she declined further, wrapping herself in scripture, and berating Sarah when her jeans were too tight, her skin showed below her neck, or when a young man happened to smile upon her while out.

"Cover yourself! I did not raise a slut to be a whore for Satan," she would rant. This level of fanaticism seemed to increase after chemotherapy robbed Mary of her hair and what was left of her health.

A home-health nurse was hired by Ed to take care of his estranged wife, and only out of love for his daughter. He knew the burden the girl carried upon her young shoulders after he left. Guilt ate him up even as he selfishly stayed away, living with his new girlfriend, and starting a new family. Meanwhile, Sarah graduated high school in her hometown of Helotes, Texas, and while friends and classmates went on to college, she remained behind, going to work at the library she'd come to love and see as a haven from the ugliness that was her life.

Her days were spent working, and her nights, caring for her mother, who'd reached stage four in her cancer. Each morning, Sarah would rise, dress for the day, and then bathe her mother, dressing her, feeding her, and making sure she took her morning medication before Vangie arrived to take over her care for the day. Most days, her mother went off on a tangent, spewing bible verses, and reminding Sarah to remain chaste and pure. She still felt a little guilty over her relief when, after prolonged illness, Mary lost her ability to speak.

The silence was a blessing.

As her mother spent more time sleeping, Sarah stayed longer at the library after hours. Vangie knew the girl needed the break. It was there, within the quiet walls of the building, after her co-workers left for the day, that she would pick out a new book, and curl up into one of the overstuffed chairs. It was also there that she first explored her sexuality. Lost in the tale of a Duke seducing the daughter of an Earl, she'd first felt desire. The book went into great detail...

Read Exposed: The Education of Sarah Brown Today!

Harvest (audiobook available free on my YouTube channel)
Hybrids
Census

Section 5 (A Harvest Trilogy Spinoff)

Angelic Hosts Series

Camael's Gift (audiobook available on my YouTube channel)
Camael's Battle (audiobook available on my YouTube channel)
Sophie's Wish
Nephilim Rising

Stand Alones

Darkest Communion (Paranormal Romance, 18+)
Waiting a Lifetime (Contemporary Romance, Mystical)
Hiring John (Romantic Comedy 18+)

Printed in the USA
CPSIA information can be obtained
at www.ICGtesting.com
LVHW042126290324
775868LV00002B/219